BRITISH BIG-SHOT

A Cocky Hero Club Novel

JH CROIX

 Created with Vellum

INTRODUCTION

British Big-Shot is a standalone story inspired by Vi Keeland and Penelope Ward's novels, Cocky Bastard and British Bedmate. It's published as part of the Cocky Hero Club world, a series of original works, written by various authors, and inspired by Keeland and Ward's *New York Times* bestselling series.

Chapter One

JASPER

"Come again?"

My solicitor lifted his head. "You cannot sell the stake in that business without a written agreement from the current owner. You're also required to visit in person and stay on-site for a month in order to obtain such an agreement."

I stared at him. "That's insane. There must be a way around that."

"I'm afraid not."

Three weeks later

. . .

I slowed to turn down the driveway. I couldn't believe I was in California visiting a winery to try to persuade a woman who had yet to reply to a single one of my emails that I wanted to sell my company's stake in her business. Sunflowers & Wine happened to be the name.

Climbing out of my car a few minutes later, I looked around. It was rather bucolic. There was a quaint barn with a rustic-looking fence with flowers spilling out of boxes mounted on the railings and winding around the posts.

I was scanning the area when I heard the sound of running. The pace didn't sound human. Turning, I was greeted by the sight of two goats wearing sweaters and running straight for me.

"What the—"

One of the little goats head-butted me in the calf. "Bloody hell! What are you doing?"

That question was directed at another goat who was chewing on the bottom of my slacks.

I shook my leg free. Exactly why I would be selling my company stake in this. Goats? What had my grandfather been thinking?

I began approaching the barn only to hear a feminine voice calling, "Jasper!"

How in the world did this woman even know my name?

Turning toward the sound of the voice, I saw a woman coming around the corner of the large barn.

"Oh!" She came to a complete stop as we stared at each other across the gravel. One of the goats bumped my calf again. "Jasper, stop it," she admonished.

I doubted that the goat would listen.

"Excuse me?" I prompted.

"I'm sorry about Jasper," she said. "He likes to butt people with his head. It's just his way of greeting you. I promise he means no harm."

"You're talking about the goat?"

The woman nodded as she began to walk toward me. A zing of electricity sizzled up my spine. This woman was startlingly beautiful. She had a riot of strawberry blond curls that glinted under the sun. She was wearing overalls, which did absolutely nothing to hide the fitted tank top underneath and her generous curves.

Stopping in front of me, she rested her hand on her hip, blinking her big brown eyes up at me. I took in the dusting of freckles on her cheeks and her thick auburn lashes. "Can I help you?" she asked.

"I'm not sure. I'm looking for Anna Lennon."

The open, welcoming expression on her face shifted slightly, tilting toward suspicion. "Whatever for?" she asked, her tone careful.

"It's a business matter." I sensed she was Anna although I didn't press the matter.

She looked away, catching her bottom lip in her teeth, denting the plump, pink surface and sending an unexpected jolt through my body.

I might've been focusing so much on work lately that I haven't had much time to date, but this kind of reaction was startling. I wasn't generally interested in women who wore overalls and spoke to goats like personal friends.

The woman's gaze swung back to me, those brown eyes narrowing. "What is the business matter?"

"I would like to speak with Ms. Lennon about it."

She let out a little huff. "I am Anna Lennon. And you are?" Her brow arched up as she stared at me.

"Jasper, Jasper West. Certainly, you're aware I own half this farm. Considering you're the other owner, I would assume you knew that."

"I'm fully aware of the business arrangement," she said, her tone sharp. "What brings you here, Jasper?"

"I'd like to sell. My grandfather's will stipulated that I needed to meet you and obtain your written agreement in order to do so. Hence, I have flown all the way from England to have this conversation with you. I assume you received my emails inquiring about this?"

This woman got under my skin, and I didn't know why. Her eyes narrowed, and she crossed her arms over her chest. I assumed she was trying to look angry, yet the motion had the unintended result of plumping up her generous breasts.

I opened my mouth to say something else only to have the other Jasper bump me with his head. It was hard enough that I lost my balance, and my foot landed in a mud puddle.

I bit back a curse. "Could you please do something about your goat?"

Chapter Two

ANNA

I had to bite the insides of my cheeks to keep from laughing. The snooty Jasper West had one of his nice shoes in a mud puddle.

Jasper, my goat—who I did *not* name after this Jasper—head-butted the other Jasper in the calf again.

Jasper lifted his head and eyed me. "Please."

God, he was still managing to be polite, and that crisp British accent did crazy things to my insides. I took a breath. "He lives here."

I didn't know why I felt so contrary, but having this British big shot show up and try to tell me what to do rankled me. My response to him also annoyed me.

Jasper West was too hot for his own good and most certainly for mine. He had rumpled black curls and piercing green eyes with a seriously built body. I'd never thought a suit was all that sexy, but on him, the fabric practically made love to his lean body. His navy suit fit his sculpted shoulders perfectly. Fortunately, or perhaps unfortunately, he wasn't wearing a tie. He had unbuttoned the top of his shirt, revealing a tantalizing glimpse of bronzed skin dusted with dark hair.

Jasper arched a brow before shaking his head. "Fine. Is there somewhere we could talk that doesn't involve the company of your goats and a mud puddle?"

I wanted to refuse, but I knew that was unreasonable. No matter how I felt about it, he did, in fact, own half the farm. This farm was all I had. When my grandmother died, I'd been startled to learn she didn't own it completely. I'd been praying Jasper West would leave me in peace, just as his grandfather had.

Since he had to have my agreement, I had some leverage, but he could certainly make it miserable for me if he chose.

"Follow me," I finally said.

Turning, I felt rather frumpy as I crossed the gravel parking area. I was in overalls and rubber boots with my hair pulled up in a messy ponytail. Meanwhile, I had a sexy British guy dripping with money in his suit following me. Le sigh.

I silently sent up a prayer of thanks to my gram. She'd taken the money Jasper's grandfather had invested and renovated the old barn into a beautiful winery. It was the shining glory of this flower and vineyard hodgepodge of a business she'd created. Though terribly curious about why Jasper's grandfather gave her all that money, I wasn't about to start by pestering him about that.

"Are you open for business?" Jasper asked as I led him through a side door into the main building at the vineyard.

"Not today," I called over my shoulder. "We're closed on Mondays. You can be assured I don't usually wear rubber boots and my overalls when we're open." I slipped out of my rubber boots, leaving them in a tray by the door before stepping into a clean pair of clogs.

"I wasn't sure you were actually traveling here," I said as I began walking down the hallway with him at my side.

"Why wouldn't I?"

"Why would you?" I countered as we stepped into the tasting area for the Sunflowers & Wine. My grandmother had named the vineyard and flower business after her two favorite things. It was that simple.

When Jasper stopped and scanned the room, I tried to see how he might view the place. The old barn had been renovated drastically. The back portion of the downstairs was where the winemaking happened and was out of view from this area. The former hayloft had been turned into a small apartment where I now lived.

This area was the front portion of the barn. The old wide plank hardwood floors had been refinished to a sheen. The former horse stalls had been transformed into a bar, but it was obvious what they once were with the front of the bar made from the refinished stall doors.

The room was pretty and airy with sunshine falling in wide shafts through the windows. Jasper's eyes, piercing and disconcerting, finally made their way back to mine. "It's lovely," he said with a subtle dip of his chin.

"What did you expect?" As soon as I spoke, I hated the sharp tone of defensiveness in my voice. Jasper didn't know I was close to broke. Even though I could argue that I didn't want him to sell, I was in over my head and drowning in debt.

"Anna, I had no idea what to expect. My grandfather passed away, and it's been about six months of sorting through his affairs. This is one of many investments he had. In order to sell, I had to come meet you, and you have to agree. I also need to stay here for a full month."

Um, what fresh hell was this?

"You have to stay here for a month?"

Jasper's eyes searched mine, and it felt like he was using an X-ray to see into my brain. I turned away, curling my arms around my waist as I crossed over to look out the windows.

Because, apparently, he was not as unsettled by me as I was by him, he followed me over, the sound of his footsteps a quiet echo in the space. When he stopped beside me, I stole a peek at him as he looked out the windows. From this side of the barn, you could see the vineyards stretching out, and then the flower fields over to one side. Although it was late afternoon, the sun was still so bright the blue background was washed out.

"It's beautiful here," he commented.

"It is."

I waited, mostly because I wasn't sure

what to say next. I couldn't believe he was supposed to spend a month here. I wanted to tell him he couldn't stay, but technically, he owned as much as I did here.

"My solicitor tells me you inherited this place from your grandmother. Were you close?" he queried.

"Yeah." My heart twinge felt a sting of grief. I missed Gram. "She's been gone a year now. She mostly raised me."

I felt Jasper's eyes on me, so I finally turned to face him. I wasn't going to be a coward. "Were you close to your grandfather?" I asked, preferring to put the focus on him.

His nod was quick and decisive. "He mostly raised me," he replied, mirroring my words.

Not sure how to guide this awkward conversation, I shifted gears. "Would you like something to eat or drink?" I finally asked, needing something to do with myself.

"That would be nice," he said, the picture of polite.

Of course, I didn't miss the questioning glint in his eyes. Screw Mr. British big shot.

I might be wearing overalls and have goats and not have enough money to get myself out of the situation I'd inherited, but I could cook. Plus, the wine-tasting kitchen was filled with hors d'oeuvres extravaganza. That was one area of the winery that paid for itself.

"Follow me." I gestured as I turned and crossed the room. I led Jasper behind the bar and into our kitchen. We didn't have a restaurant, but we had wine-tasting events every week. We had those cute little sandwiches and dips and gourmet cheeses and crackers and more. All of it sourced locally, of course.

This area of the barn was a little more comfortable for me and not so fancy. When I glanced over to see Jasper standing beside the counter and surveying the room, I almost laughed. We were a pair of opposites, that was for sure. Me in my overalls, and him in his suit.

He was quiet. The kitchen had all stainless-steel appliances, purchased with the money from his grandfather. A small table sat in the corner where I grabbed breakfast down here on occasion.

"Coffee?" I asked.

Jasper shook his wrist lightly before pushing up his sleeve and glancing at his watch. "I'd rather taste the wine if you don't mind."

God, everything he said came out so crisp. He gave off a grumpy, annoyed vibe as though he couldn't wait to shake off this experience. Whatever. We had amazing wine. My grandmother made magic with it, and I learned everything I knew from her.

"Of course," I said with a tight smile. "Would you like red or white wine?"

"I'll take a red."

After fetching some wine, I pulled out one of the hors d'oeuvre trays left over from last night's tasting. Crossing the room, I set the tray down with two plates and uncorked the wine.

Jasper lifted the wine bottle. "I admit to enjoying wine, but I've never been to an official wine tasting. Is this when people usually smell it?" he asked as I handed over the wineglass.

I shrugged, adjusting a strap on my overalls. "Some people do. As much as I love wine, I don't tend to bother."

He responded with an arch of his brow before pouring some wine into both glasses and taking a swallow from his. My eyes lingered on the motion of his throat. He was too handsome. The shadow of his stubble highlighted the sharp lines of his jaw. Of course, his cheekbones were impeccable as well, almost elegant in their bold angles. His eyes were intense. The only thing that wasn't model-worthy was his nose, which was a little crooked.

"Did you break your nose?" As usual, my words tumbled out before I could snatch them back.

He stared at me for a beat, his lips twitching slightly. "Yes. Playing rugby in school."

"Do you still play?"

"Here and there for fun only. It's not something I have much time for."

"I suppose you're busy chasing down your investments and trying to persuade them to sell. How many of these arrangements did your grandfather leave behind?" I asked, my voice a little sharper than I intended.

Jasper took another swallow of wine. "This is delicious." I felt a flush of pride before he continued. "To your question, this is the only one. I don't know why he purchased half of this business. I don't even know if I'll know after I spend a month here."

"Where do you plan to stay?" My heart banged against my ribs, and my belly flipped over when he gave me another one of those intense looks. I didn't really like him, yet my body was ignoring my mind. He was just all too yummy.

"The will stipulates that I stay at the actual vineyard. I thought perhaps you could let me know what my options were here."

Options?

There were no options. This barn had an upstairs where I stayed, the greenhouse, and then the barn where my goats and chickens lived. Somehow, I doubted he'd appreciate the limited options I had.

I took a gulp of my wine and swallowed too much at once. I almost choked, splattering wine on my tank top and the table.

Jasper stayed quiet, simply arching a brow as he reached for a napkin and leaned over to quickly wipe up the wine on the table. Everything he did was smooth and measured. Meanwhile, I snatched a napkin and dabbed it pointlessly at my shirt.

When I lifted my eyes again and found his watching me, the heat of his gaze was like licks of fire on my skin. That had to be my imagination. My nipples didn't think so. They perked up, ready to say hello to the hot British guy.

"Where do you live?" he asked politely.

I pointed toward the ceiling.

"Upstairs?"

I nodded.

"Is there anywhere else to stay here?"

"With the goats and the chickens in the barn." I figured I might as well be honest.

"So I'm to be treated like a goat. Lovely."

I narrowed my eyes at him. "Forgive me, but I didn't know about the stipulation, and I don't even know what to think. I suppose you can stay in the guest bedroom upstairs," I said stiffly.

Jasper watched me quietly. All kinds of things passed through his eyes, none of which I knew how to interpret.

"That will suffice," he finally replied.

"Suffice?"

"Be adequate," he clarified.

"I know what suffice means," I muttered as I took a more careful swallow of my wine. "This is really strange."

"It certainly is, but it's what we have to do. I assume you'd like to buy me out."

I stared at him, desperately hoping he couldn't see the worry spinning inside me. When he dipped his chin, lasering me with his eyes, I knew he could.

Jasper leaned back in his chair to stare at the ceiling before leveling me with his eyes again. "Bloody hell. You're in financial trouble, aren't you?"

I swallowed and nodded slowly. "All I did was inherit the financial trouble. But I love this place, and I have a plan to turn it around. I certainly don't have money to buy you out, and I'd prefer not to be saddled with an owner I don't know."

"You just met me."

"Obviously, I'm aware of that. Your grandfather was very fair and easy to deal with, so I can only hope you would be the same. Even if you are kind of a grumpy snob."

Chapter Three

JASPER

I stared at Anna's retreating form. Despite the rather shapeless overalls, she couldn't hide the lush curve of her hips. I also couldn't erase the sight of the wine splattered on her fitted tank top. More specifically, I couldn't forget the way her tight nipples pressed against the damp cotton.

Things were tight, all right. When I began to turn and close the door to the room she'd just shown me, I heard her footsteps stop. She looked over her shoulder. "Bathroom's right there. We have to share."

"Thank you," I managed.

She disappeared through another doorway. Closing the door to the guest bedroom, I took stock of my accommodations for the month. Although this space above the winery wasn't too large, it was very nice. The floors were freshly finished, and the walls appeared to have fresh paint in soft cream. The entire space felt light and airy with a giant window that looked out over the vineyard. Now the moon was rising, casting a silvery glow over the fields. As I looked out the windows, I saw a light illuminating the area behind this barn.

I watched curiously as Anna emerged. The goats appeared, following her across the lawn into a smaller barn. Turning away, I looked down at the dried mud on my slacks and slowly shook my head.

I had *no* idea what my grandfather had been thinking. I knew he had a mischievous streak a mile wide and had no problem meddling in anyone's life, not if he cared about them. He was definitely meddling from the grave with this plan. I'd thought I'd show up here and discover the owner thought the entire plan was as ridiculous as I did. No such luck.

The look of worry when Anna heard I expected she'd want to buy me out had elicited unaccountable twinges of guilt. This was a business decision. I didn't need to feel guilty about some American girl whose grandmother had run up too much debt.

"Bloody hell," I muttered to myself.

Knowing she was probably feeding the goats outside, I went to the bathroom to wash up. Not much later, I was marveling at how comfortable the bed was with a light-weight down quilt and soft cotton sheets. The space was a far cry from the massive bedroom suite I had in my flat in London, but the bed was more comfortable than my own. It would definitely suffice.

The moment I thought that word, I almost chuckled out loud, recalling Anna's reaction earlier. No doubt she was sharp as a tack, but I just didn't know how we were going to get along for an entire month.

Chapter Four

ANNA

I nudged Jasper, the goat, with my knee. "Back up. Tinker Bell needs some food too."

Jasper obligingly backed away from Tinker Bell's small pile of hay and returned to the one on the other side of the stall. They didn't have their sweaters on this morning. Jasper was named because he looked like a jasper stone with a part of his rump spotted. Tinker Bell was a prissy little girl and pure white. Together, they brought me plenty of smiles.

After they were settled with their food, I went to gather the eggs from the chickens before returning to the kitchen. It was early, the sun not even cresting the horizon yet. I paused by the door into the kitchen to turn and look out over the vineyard.

Taking a deep breath of the fresh early morning air, I let it out with a slow sigh. I loved it here. Now, I had the other Jasper to worry about, and I didn't know what to do. Every time I woke from my restless sleep last night, which seemed to be every hour, I fretted over what he might decide to do and worried about money.

The sky was stained tangerine and red, and I knew the sun would inch its way above the horizon soon. For now, everything was quiet, well, except for Randy the rooster. He took the moment to announce his presence.

After letting myself quietly into the kitchen, I tied an apron around my waist. I was dressed a little nicer today than my overalls and boots yesterday. And not just because Jasper was here. We were open today. Mondays were flower market days when customers could come and pick from the flowers on the farm. We had some ready to go and other areas where they could pick from the wildflowers. I took a quick glance at the clock and saw it was approaching six a.m. My small collection of staff would be arriving around seven.

I was fretting over whether I should let

Jasper know about the schedule, or just leave him to his own devices. It was all very weird because he technically owned half of this place.

After rinsing the eggs off and leaving them on a towel to dry, I started a pot of coffee before hurrying out to the greenhouse to make sure everything was ready. I was in the middle of putting together clusters of pink daisies when I heard footsteps. Turning, I found Jasper approaching. He wasn't wearing his suit this morning. Unfortunately for me, one look at him caused my pulse to do a happy dance and take off running as if we had a race to win.

Jasper's hair was damp, and he wore a button-down shirt with the sleeves rolled up and a pair of jeans. He had a coffee cup in hand, and I felt a small sense of satisfaction about that. I had no idea why.

"Good morning," he said with a dip of his head.

"Good morning," I returned, a little breathlessly.

He stopped beside me, and it instantly felt too close. His presence was unsettling for me. His perceptive eyes scanned the greenhouse before they made their way back to me. "Is this where you grow all the flowers?"

"Some of them." I waved generally over my shoulder. "We have a small field out there. We use the greenhouse for ones that need more babying. We sell a lot of wildflowers, and those all grow outside," I explained. "I wasn't sure what I should tell you about our schedule. Mondays are what we call our flower market. We sell wildflowers and perennials as well as floral arrangements." I tied a purple ribbon around the cluster of pink daisies before tucking them in a vase with fresh water. "I'm about all set for the morning. Would you like some breakfast?"

"I'm certainly not going to turn down food. Do you serve food to customers?" he asked, falling in step beside me as I began walking out of the greenhouse.

"Not for the flower side of the business. When we do wine tastings, we serve hors d'oeuvres, but that's it. I can't even imagine trying to do official food service on top of everything else."

Once we were in the kitchen, I tied an apron around my waist. "I have fresh eggs. How does an omelet sound?"

"Delicious. Can I help?"

Startled at his question, I paused for a moment before replying, "Um, I guess you could shred some cheese."

It felt strange having him help. I felt like I should be waiting on him, which didn't really make sense. But then, none of this made sense. Here we were, the two grandchildren of the people who'd owned this farm. I still didn't even know why my grandmother had the business partnership with his grandfather. All I knew was she'd done a summer abroad in England when she was in college and met him. In my few conversations with him over the phone and via email, Jasper's grandfather had told me they had a special friendship and nothing more.

I quickly chopped some fresh tarragon to pair with mushrooms, spinach, and cheese for the omelets. After Jasper shredded the cheese, I added fresh milk.

"Is all of this right here from the farm?" he asked, watching as I whisked the mixture in a bowl.

Glancing up, I nodded. "It's fresh goat milk. I don't always have it on hand, but when I do, I use it."

Jasper nodded. "I hope you don't mind that I helped myself to some coffee earlier."

"Of course not." Once I had the first omelet in the pan, I got my own cup of coffee.

Not much later, we were seated at the

small round table in the corner of the kitchen. Jasper took a bite of his omelet and closed his eyes, letting out a sound of satisfaction. Opening his eyes, he stared at me. "This is amazing."

I almost laughed and felt a flush crest on my cheeks. "Thank you. Fresh ingredients do make everything better."

After I cleaned my plate, I glanced over at him. "I'm not sure what you'd like to do today. Obviously, you own half of this place, so you're welcome to do as you please."

He finished a sip of coffee. "I was thinking I could start by taking a look at the accounts."

Suddenly feeling defensive, I wanted to tell him no. They were a mess, and I didn't know what to do. Actually, I knew what to do. I needed money to fix the mess. I'd yet to magically find it.

"Maybe it would be more fun to—"

Jasper leveled me with a look. "I need to see what the situation is. I'm sure you understand."

I swallowed and willed the sick churning in my stomach to stop. "Of course. My grandmother lost a lot of money during the recession a while ago. She never quite recovered."

Jasper's eyes searched mine. I hated the

feel of heat climbing up my cheeks and the way my pulse kept going a little crazy around him. "Understood."

"Isn't it something we could do together?" I pressed. "I'd feel better about that."

"I suppose, but I'd prefer not to wait."

I leaped up from my chair, snatching his empty plate along with mine. "Fine. My laptop is upstairs. It's on the coffee table. The password is sunshine."

Jasper stood. "You don't need to tell me the password. You can log me in."

"There's nothing personal on that laptop. My grandmother used spreadsheets to track everything. Feel free to take a look in her filing cabinet. That's in the corner of the room upstairs."

I was furious, and I didn't know exactly why. I wanted him to give me a little time to absorb the fact that he probably wasn't going to give me any choice about this. Either I had an unpleasant and uneasy partnership with him, or he sold his share. Since I couldn't afford to buy him out, I'd be dealing with yet another unknown business partner.

I put the plates in the dishwasher and hurried out. "I'll be outside if you need anything."

I didn't tell Jasper I'd emailed the attorney listed in one of the emails his grandfather had sent. There was no point. I'd asked if it was true that Jasper needed to spend a month here.

That's correct. Odd though it may seem, that was the stipulation in his grandfather's will. Please be aware if Jasper wants to sell, you are not required to agree.

The succinct and clear reply didn't change anything.

Chapter Five

JASPER

"Can you please tell me what my grandfather was thinking?"

I had my phone on speaker as I scrolled through the haphazard accounting system, if it could even be called a system, Anna's grandmother used.

"I'm afraid I can't tell you. I have a letter for you that's only to be opened after you have spent your month in California," Benjamin, my grandfather's solicitor, explained.

"He's not here. I miss him dearly, and I would trade him being alive for this situation, even if I knew it was coming. But you work for me now. Can't I see the letter now?"

"Jasper, I'm fully aware of that. However, you don't seem to be aware of my obligations as an executor of his estate. I can't change the guidelines simply because the living person bequeathed the resources would like me to do so."

"Oh, hell," I muttered under my breath.

"Your frustration is noted," Benjamin said crisply. "Is there anything else I can do for you at the moment?"

"Just one thing. Please ask my accountant to review any of the records my grandfather had on this business partnership. Have him email them directly to my personal email, please."

I had enough sense to know Anna was being mostly honest about what had happened. Although I didn't know her well, my gut told me she didn't have it in her to be dishonest. Despite the not particularly organized state of her grandmother's spreadsheets, it was clear the business was in the black up until the recession a decade ago but then hadn't recovered after that. Interestingly, the partnership with my grandfather was finalized after the recession, but he'd lent her money before that on two occasions. I was far too curious about the nature of their relationship.

I stood from the chair where I'd set myself up in the loft apartment. The windows offered a stunning view of the vineyard and the flower fields. I had taken advantage of the small desk Anna had situated to face out the windows. At the moment, there were throngs of people milling about in the flower fields and coming in and out of the greenhouse.

There was no doubt this farm had promise and potential. I couldn't believe I was even marginally contemplating maintaining this investment. Anna's strawberry blond hair glinted under the sun as she walked through the parking area, talking animatedly with an elderly couple. Her smile was bright as she handed over a bouquet of wildflowers and waved them off when they tried to pay her.

"Oh, for fuck's sake. Maybe you're still in debt because you don't take money from perfectly good paying customers," I said to absolutely no one.

Running a hand through my hair, I spun on my heel, surveying this small space. The loft apartment had a tall ceiling, and Anna had plants in each corner. The big, fluffy ferns were little explosions of greenery. I'd never had a plant in my life.

I may only have known her for just about twenty-four hours, but the space felt so much like her. There were touches of whimsy with vibrant glass vases with flowers, a painting of a goat wearing a hot pink sweater with hearts all over it, and a few scarves thrown over the back of the comfy-looking sofa.

The loft was comprised of mostly open space—a living room with a desk and a filing cabinet tucked in the corner, which I supposed would count as the office. The wide island counter in the back served as a divider between this space and the kitchen. Constructed from what looked like a refinished barn door, it had been polished to a sheen with a glossy finish. The stools surrounding the island had deep purple upholstery and butterflies carved in the wooden backs of the seats. Directly to one side were three doors—the bathroom, the guest room, and what I presumed was Anna's bedroom.

I didn't consider myself a nosy person, but apparently that didn't hold when it came to Anna. As I crossed the room and lightly pressed two fingers on the wooden door to push it open, I told myself I technically owned half this place and it wasn't personal curiosity that compelled me to peek into her bedroom.

Looking through that doorway, I found myself annoyed with my curiosity. Her bed was a massive wrought iron feminine concoction. She actually had a canopy of gauzy sheer fabric. The bed was piled high with pillows and a massive cream-colored fluffy quilt with an eyelet fringe around the bottom.

On the one hand, the woman I met yesterday in her rubber boots and overalls without a lick of make-up on her face had a hint of tomboy to her. Perhaps more than a hint. Yet looking at this room, her feminine side screamed out at me. She was definitely a woman of contrast.

And I wanted her. It made no sense, not at all.

Every time I thought of trying to persuade her to agree to let me sell my half of the business, I felt a twinge of guilt, which was completely crazy. I'd obviously gone bonkers. I was a businessman, and this was purely business.

Yet much about it had nothing to do with business. My grandfather was a businessman, and not one of his other business collaborations had this bizarre arrangement tied to the estate. For crying out loud, I had to be her roommate for an entire month to even consider asking her to allow me to sell.

Flying out here, I'd thought perhaps I'd meet her, and she'd realize how ridiculous the entire arrangement was and sign off on it anyway. Having met her, I now knew I'd have to badger her into it, and that might not even work.

With a mental shake, I exited her bedroom and decided to go see more of the business. By late afternoon, I'd been given a tour of the winery. I meandered through the fields, if only because I was curious. The crowds for the flowers were beginning to thin out when I saw a couple climbing out of their car, followed by a goat. A bloody goat.

Chapter Six

ANNA

"Hey, Anna," Aubrey called as she crossed the parking area with her pet goat trotting along beside her.

At that moment, I sensed Jasper's presence. Glancing over my shoulder, I saw him standing inside the gate that led from the parking area into the flower greenhouse. My skin prickled, and my belly did a little flip. Even from here, it felt like his eyes were peeling away all my layers. That *had* to be my imagination.

Looking away, I smiled brightly at Aubrey and Chance. "How's it going?" Chance asked, ever cheerful. Chance was a retired professional soccer player from Australia. With his fit body, copper-brown hair, and blue eyes, he was hard not to notice, yet he only ever had eyes for Aubrey, who was a looker all on her own with her auburn curls and wide green eyes. All good looks aside, they were good friends to me, and I was glad I'd gotten to know them.

I'd met Aubrey and Chance by chance. No pun intended. They liked to travel with their pet goat, Pixy, but they'd needed to fly somewhere and called the farm because they heard we had goats and wondered if he could stay here temporarily. Thus, a friendship was born. Every so often, I went out of town, and it was nice to know someone local who I could ask to help in a pinch for taking care of the goats and the chickens.

"Hey there, how's Pixy?"

"He's good. He's getting old," Chance offered.

I looked down at Pixy. He was quite the character. He bumped his head against my knees, and I leaned over to pet him. "He looks healthy as can be," I offered as I straightened. "What brings you out here today?"

"I was hoping you had a fresh batch of my favorite raspberry mead," Chance replied.

"We sure do. Would you like to come in and get it?"

They followed me along the path into the winery. "Looks busy today," Aubrey commented. "That's good, right?"

"It certainly is." Aubrey was aware of my financial stressors. "Where's CJ?" I asked, referring to their young son.

"Chance's sister has him for the day. Who's the hottie standing at the gate?" she teased under her breath.

"He's actually the son of my grandmother's friend who owns half of this whole place," I whispered. "It's a long story, so I'll have to explain later. Please be nice."

Chance hadn't heard any of this and strolled right on past Jasper who turned as I reached him. "How's it going?" I asked, trying not to be nervous.

My lady parts did a little happy dance and my pulse took off the moment Jasper's green eyes met mine. "It's going well. You've had a busy day."

"She's always busy," Aubrey chimed in at my side. Pixy trotted off when he saw Jasper and Tinker Bell in their small field nearby.

Jasper looked at her, smiling politely. Gesturing between them, I said, "Aubrey, this is Jasper West. Jasper, this is my friend Aubrey."

Chance turned back and approached us, his ever-curious eyes bouncing among the three of us. Jasper looked at him quizzically. Chance had been pretty famous during his soccer career, but ever since he and Aubrey had settled down, they lived a fairly quiet life with their young son.

Chance cast Jasper an easy grin. "I'm Chance. Nice to meet you," he said, holding his hand out.

"Have I seen you before?" Jasper asked as he shook his hand.

Chance shrugged. "Maybe. I used to play soccer professionally."

"Ah," Jasper said, that single syllable still managing to sound so very British and kind of haughty.

"They're here for some fresh raspberry mead," I explained as we began walking into the winery.

Jasper nodded. "Eloise mentioned she was finishing a batch this morning. She told me I had to have your permission to taste any."

Eloise had been with the winery when my grandmother started it and helped run the business. I felt my cheeks heat. "I'll have to explain to her that you actually own half this place. I haven't had time to talk with the staff since you arrived. Today is one of my busier days."

We soon stepped into the cool front section of the winery. Since we weren't doing a tasting today, it was quiet. Aubrey caught my eye as Jasper paused to study the chalkboard behind the bar. I knew she was curious, but I didn't have much to share about Jasper. Other than the fact that he'd shown up and was about to ruin my life.

I was tense and stressed and worried and anxious, and wondering if any other words could be used to describe the same thing. I shoved those feelings deep down inside.

"Come on back." I gestured for them to follow me into the non-public area.

When I passed Jasper, I couldn't help but notice his great ass. Every inch of him was muscular, and his ass was no exception. My hands tingled with the urge to touch him.

I wasn't crazy, though, so I forced my eyes away. Eloise smiled as we came into the back. "Oh, hey, y'all," she called, her Southern twang soothing to my rattled nerves.

"Please tell us the mead is ready," Chance said, lowering his voice to a somber tone.

Eloise brushed her gray curls off her shoulders as she grinned. "Absolutely. If there's one thing I can handle, it's a schedule. As long as the ingredients follow my wishes, that is." She looked over toward me. "I forgot to tell you, the couple who wanted to come out tonight to review some options for their wedding had to cancel because the bride-to-be has a stomach bug."

"Did they reschedule?" I asked.

"For next week. The only problem is, I had already cooked those pizzas they wanted to taste. I hope you don't mind if I take some home for the grandkids." Her blue eyes twinkled when she smiled.

"Of course not. Do you two want to stay for dinner?" I asked as I look toward Aubrey and Chance.

Having them here would alleviate some of the intensity of Jasper. I did *not* know how to deal with my brand-new roommate under these strange circumstances.

"Hell, yeah," Chance said with a grin. "We already have a babysitter tonight."

Aubrey laughed softly, nudging him in the side with her elbow. "We do. We would love to. Are you going to join us, Jasper?" she asked, turning her pretty smile on him.

Jasper had been standing quietly, his eyes perusing the rows of wine bottles. Turning, he nodded. "Of course. I'm here anyway."

"Oh, are you staying here?" Aubrey queried.

Chapter Seven

JASPER

Aubrey's wide eyes stared at me. She was practically bubbling over with curiosity. "Yes, I am," I replied.

Anna looked at me, her cheeks going a little pink. Bloody hell. All that woman had to do was look at me, and she sent a little jolt of lust sizzling through my body. Too bad she hated me.

"It's kind of weird how Jasper ended up staying here," she began. "Let's go out front. I'll grab a few pizzas and something to drink. Do you want some of the mead tonight?"

"I'm driving, so I'll take water," Chance said, holding his hand up.

"I'll have some," Aubrey replied as we all

turned and followed Anna out to the front of the winery.

When Anna turned to go get the pizzas, she literally shooed me away with her hand when I offered to help. I sat down on one of the stools at the counter at the bar. "How did you end up here after playing soccer?" I asked conversationally.

"I fell in love." Chance looped his arm around Aubrey shoulders and leaned over to drop a kiss on the side of her neck. Her skin went pink.

"We met on a trip," she explained. "Chance's sister lives in the area. It took some time, but we eventually found our way together."

"Ah, I see. Mind if I ask how you ended up with a goat?"

"We found him. He fell over in the road, and we stopped to pick him up," Chance explained.

At that moment, Anna returned. She passed around plates and then set two pizzas on the counter. When I looked down at them, my mouth actually watered.

"Oh my. What are these flavors?" Aubrey asked as she reached for one of the bottles of wine Anna set in the middle of the bar.

"Well, these are for a wedding sampler.

Each pizza has four flavors on it. This one has pear with goat cheese and a honey drizzle. This is prosciutto, fresh tomato, and basil. This is good ole pepperoni, and this last one is a variation on Greek with the olives we grow right here," Anna explained as she gestured to the different sections on each pizza. "Does anybody need water or anything?"

"I do," Chance reminded her. "Much as I would like to partake of the fresh raspberry mead, I'm going to wait."

Anna hurried off, returning with a pitcher of water and four glasses. We settled in to eat, and it was truly divine. I was discovering that while I might be living in a rustic area, at least the food was going to be amazing. My omelet this morning currently ranked as the single best breakfast I'd ever had. This was now the best pizza I'd ever tasted.

Over dinner, Anna actually relaxed since the first time I'd met her. It was clear she and Aubrey were close friends. They chatted about local things and the oddities of taking care of goats. Chance told me about his online videos.

There was only one problem.

Anna undid her ponytail and her glorious strawberry curls fell around her shoulders. Her breasts strained at the fabric of her button-down shirt, stretching it slightly, and I wanted to undo that top button with my teeth. The more mead she drank, the more relaxed she became. I found a relaxed Anna to be downright intoxicating. She bordered on tipsy by the time dinner was done, but thankfully, she didn't need to drive anywhere.

When Chance and Aubrey were ready to leave, we had to help them find Pixy, so I found myself wandering around the barn, calling out for a goat. I found one, but it was Jasper, and he head-butted me right in the shins again.

I looked down at him. "Really?"

Anna approached with the proper goat at her side. I supposed she was a goat charmer.

"That's a sign of affection. I think he likes you. You do share his name, after all," she commented.

Aubrey's laughter reached my ears. "Oh, my God! I didn't even think about that. That's hysterical. That's a sign, you know?"

"A sign?" Anna asked, her brows hitching up and practically flying off her hairline.

"I don't know what the sign is. I'm just saying it's got to be one. What are the chances that a man by the name of Jasper would show up and your favorite goat by the same name would love him?"

"I don't have favorites," Anna protested, looking truly horrified at this thought.

"We all have favorites. Jasper's cute and affectionate. Tinker Bell is more standoffish and kind of princessy," Aubrey observed.

I had to agree with her on that point although I chose not to share that opinion. I didn't want to offend Anna over her goats.

"Nice to meet you, Jasper," Aubrey called as she climbed in the car a few moments later.

Chance lifted his hand in a friendly wave. "Hopefully, we'll see you again while you're visiting."

I waved as they drove off. When I looked back, Anna was nowhere to be found, but then I heard her talking. To what, or rather who, I didn't know. Following the sound of her voice, I found her chatting with the chickens. "And he's going to ruin everything. What should I do, girls?"

She stumbled slightly as she closed the gate to their small enclosure. I crossed over to her quickly, catching her by the elbow to steady her.

"I'm not going to ruin everything, Anna, okay? We'll figure it out."

She walked quietly alongside me before

coming to an abrupt stop just under an archway decorated with strung lights.

"You don't understand," she said softly. "And why do you have to be so handsome?" This was accompanied by a poke in my chest with her index finger.

"Why don't we just call it a night? You've had a busy day, and I'm sure you're tired. Now definitely isn't the time to worry about what's going happen with my share. Plus, we have a month."

Anna's wide brown eyes held mine, and everything in my body tightened. This woman was making me crazy. I didn't know how else to explain the intensity of my physical response to her. Her palm fell fully against my chest, and my heart lunged toward it. She took a shuddery breath.

"I think you should kiss me," she announced.

Just then, she leaned up toward me before wobbling and almost knocking us both over. Catching my balance, I held her against me.

"I think not," I finally replied. "We've had a bit too much to drink."

"Of course, you'd say that. You're stuffy, snooty, and a prude."

With that, she nudged me hard in the side with her elbow and walked off.

Chapter Eight

ANNA

When I woke, my head was pounding. Ugh. I slowly opened one eye and then the other, squinting at the sunlight angling through my bedroom window. My eyes landed on the clock.

"Oh, fuck. Ouch!" I exclaimed, cradling my forehead with my hand after trying to sit up too abruptly.

I had a hangover, and it was all Jasper's fault. The moment I recalled Jasper, a wave of mortification slammed into me. I tried to kiss him last night. And he turned me down.

I'd gotten drunk, probably because I was so anxious and stressed about him being here, inspecting his half of the business. The whole situation just made me feel sick and worried and foolish. When Gram had died last year, somehow Jasper's grandfather—whom I'd never met in person—had felt like this distant but warm and caring figure.

He'd always replied jovially in our correspondence over email and been supportive and encouraging. When I received notice that he had passed away from the lawyer handling his estate, I felt sad even though I'd never met the man. The attorney had assured me there would be no sale without my written agreement.

I didn't know what I'd imagined would happen, but it definitely wasn't Jasper showing up all British and sexy and making me feel judged.

I took a longing look at the clock, hoping maybe I'd read it wrong the first time. No such luck. It was still five-thirty a.m. I needed to get up.

The simple act of sitting up in my bed and swinging my feet to the floor had me feeling as if a cruel devil had a hammer inside my skull. I prayed Jasper was asleep although I doubted it. He would be up bright and early again to torture me. Now, I got to be embarrassed on top of everything else.

Wrapping my robe around me, I tiptoed to my door, annoyed that I even had to worry about dealing with someone else in my space. What in the world had his grandfather been thinking by insisting Jasper had to stay here for a month?

After I leaned my ear against the door and detected no sound, I opened it slowly and peered out. A quick scan revealed the living room and kitchen to be free of Jasper, and the guest room door was closed.

I tiptoed out and hurried into the bathroom. After I downed some ibuprofen to get rid of my headache, I climbed into the shower, hoping the steam would help me feel a little bit better before I had to face the day. Thank goodness today wasn't one of the flower days.

Once I was done showering, I tied the sash to my robe and tiptoed out, crossing into the small kitchenette to start the coffee. Just as I was turning to tiptoe into my bedroom, Jasper's door opened.

He stepped out, and my jaw almost hit the floor. Dear God. It wasn't fair that he was so handsome. His dark hair was rumpled from sleep, and the shadow of stubble on his jaw only made him even sexier. His sweatpants hung low on his hips, and he didn't have a shirt on. I repeat: He. Did. Not. Have. A. Shirt. On.

It felt as if perhaps an emergency siren should go off alerting me to the fact that I needed to flee. *Danger, danger. Too much British hotness entering the room.*

He scrubbed a hand over his face and then looked my way. Even sleepy, even with bedhead, the moment his eyes landed on me, his gaze sharpened, and he looked completely alert.

My toes pressed against the cool hardwood floor. They literally wanted to curl because he was so hot. Gah! He had a dusting of dark hair on his chest that narrowed to a little trail. His body was all lean, rangy muscle. My mouth practically watered. It didn't matter that I had a headache. I just wanted to lick him all over.

Jasper's eyes swept from my face down to my toes, painted bright purple, and then back up. I felt hot and flushed, and butterflies burst to life in my belly.

I swallowed. "Good morning," I finally managed, the words coming out too breathless.

"Good morning, Anna. How are you feeling?" he asked in that polite, crisp accent.

I took a breath, not getting all that much air in with my lungs rebelling against my effort to be in control. They were all like, *Hell no, he makes us breathless, and we can't do our job.*

"Um, okay." I gestured vaguely in the direction of the coffee pot. "I made some coffee. It should be ready in a few minutes. I'm just going to get dressed."

I practically ran past him into my bedroom, wincing when I closed the door too loudly. I leaned my back against it, trying to catch my breath.

"Get a grip," I whispered to myself. "He probably forgot you tried to kiss him."

I wanted to hide in my bedroom. But I wasn't a coward, and I actually had things to do. My stomach let out a growl, also reminding me I was starving.

Pulling out a T-shirt and a clean pair of overalls, I deliberately decided to go with the farm-girl look. I didn't need to be sexy for him, not at all.

A few minutes later, I was pouring myself a cup of coffee when he reappeared from the bathroom, blessedly dressed with damp hair. My body couldn't decide if it was disappointed he wasn't shirtless or relieved he was fully clothed so I didn't do anything stupid like last night.

I had a bagel in the toaster. Looking over, I asked, "Would you like a bagel?"

"I'd love one," he replied.

"Coffee is ready," I added as I turned and reached out to get a mug from the cabinet.

Jasper was quiet until I handed him the bagel with a small bowl of cream cheese. "Let me guess, you made this cream cheese and seasoned it with fresh herbs." His lips were quirking with a smile when I looked over, and I felt a flash of heat flood my cheeks.

"Yes to both."

After he spread some cream cheese on a bagel, he took a bite and let out a moan. My belly spun in flips. I certainly hoped I could get a handle on my body in the next few days. Because I had a month ahead of me with Jasper here, and I didn't want to be feeling this crazy inside the whole time.

"You're going to spoil me," he said after he finished chewing.

"I doubt that," I replied.

We ate quietly at the table together. After I stood and carried our plates to the sink, he spoke. "I looked at the accounting spreadsheets. The recession did hit your grandmother hard. She had a solid business, so it's just a matter of getting back on even footing."

Turning, I leaned my hips against the counter, curling my hands around the edge.

"That's what I thought. Since she died, it's just taking a little while for me to get up to speed. I'm sure I can figure it out."

I wanted to ask him questions, but the most pressing one was whether he was going to push me to agree to let him sell his half. I didn't really want to have that conversation just yet.

"I, um, need to get to work. I have to feed the chickens and check on the goats," I muttered. "I guess I'll see you later."

He watched me as I pushed away from the counter, then surprised me when he stood from the table. "Why don't I help?"

Startled, I swung back toward him. He shrugged lightly. "I have to be here for a month. I'm not one who enjoys being idle."

I stared at him, actually biting my bottom lip to keep from blurting out a refusal. Because that was rude. He was offering to help, and I could always use help, but I also needed to be nice. Being nice might increase the chances that he would just go back to England in his suit and be a silent partner like his grandfather.

"Sure," I finally bit out.

Chapter Nine

JASPER

Anna was tense. "Right there," she said, pointing at a stack of hay bales. "It's alfalfa. It's their favorite."

"How much?"

"Two sections. You'll see as soon as you cut the ties. It'll fall off in sections."

She turned away, opening a bin against the wall and scooping out some kind of grain. We were in the barn where the chickens and goats were. This was apparently the feed room, as she'd explained when we walked in. Hay was stacked against one wall with bins mounted on the other.

"What do you feed the chickens?" I asked, determined to be friendly despite her frosty demeanor.

"Leftover vegetables and the regular feed along with some cracked corn. That's kind of a treat for them," she explained.

I followed her out. "You can just toss the alfalfa into their stall." She pointed over her shoulder, not even looking back at me.

It was all fine and well for her to ignore me because I was having enough trouble keeping my reaction to her in check. She was back in her overalls, but this time, she wore a V-neck T-shirt underneath.

Unfortunately for me, Anna yanked on my chain big time. With zero effort, she had my entire body humming. It was a constant low vibration of electricity. Her strawberry blond curls were pulled up into a messy pony-tail. Her T-shirt didn't do a damn thing to hide the lush curves of her breasts and only drew attention to the shadowed valley between.

I stopped by the goats' stall. Jasper poked his nose through the wooden slats and nipped at my knee. "Hey, easy there," I said. "I've got your breakfast. You'll be surprised to know it's not my jeans."

I tossed the hay into the stall and watched as they quickly began happily jumping on it. Jasper was a little guy with black spots on his white rump and a big black splotch on his chest. Tinker Bell was all white and a little zippy as she moved around the stall and tried to beat Jasper with her speed of chewing.

Curious about the chickens, I walked over to find Anna had stepped outside and opened the gate. She scattered the cracked corn on the ground and filled the feeder with the other food.

"How's the water doing?" she asked the chickens, I supposed.

When she bent over, I had an unfortunately awesome view of her round bottom. Although her overalls were loose, they couldn't hide all her curves. She straightened and turned, her eyes widening when she saw me there. "Oh. I didn't realize you wanted to help with the chickens. I'm getting the eggs now."

She picked up a set of gloves on the shelf just inside the chicken coop. "Mandy is broody," she explained.

I had no idea what she was talking about, so I just followed her into the small fenced area. The chicken I presumed to be Mandy was copper colored and was sitting in one of the boxes filled with hay. The moment Anna attempted to reach out to her, Mandy pecked at her hand.

Anna spoke in a soothing voice. "Easy, girl. I'm just getting your eggs. You can lay some more for tomorrow."

After Anna slipped out four eggs, Mandy hopped onto the ground and hurried out to eat with the rest of the chickens. The only rooster eyed me from where he stood on top of an overturned plastic bucket. He let out a call, and I could've sworn he gave me a defensive look, almost as if to say, "See, I'm in charge here."

Anna glanced over to him and laughed. "He's a man, Randy, but he doesn't want your girls."

"Oh, so I'm not crazy?" I asked as we walked out.

"Well, I wouldn't know the answer to that," she said when she stopped and looked up at me, holding the eggs carefully in her hands.

"I thought he was giving me a look. Your rooster, that is."

"Oh, for sure. He's very protective of his girls, and you're a man. He knows it."

I followed her back into the winery kitchen. "Would you like another omelet?"

she asked as she rinsed the eggs in the sink and set them in a bowl.

"You can be rest assured I won't refuse any food you offer me. I've discovered you're an incredible cook."

Anna's cheeks went pink, and she turned away quickly. "Omelet, it is." She strode over to the refrigerator and peered inside. "How do fresh red peppers with feta and mushrooms sound for it?"

"Excellent."

She got to cooking, and I wondered how to busy myself. She clearly didn't like being alone with me. I was going to stick this month out because I planned to sell, and I had to persuade her to go along with it.

The door to the back opened, and Eloise came through the door. "Good morning. So nice to see you again, Jasper. I understand from Anna that we'll get the pleasure of your company all month." Eloise had a twang to her voice, and I guessed it to be Southern.

"Good morning as well. I'll try to be of service while I'm here," I replied.

Smoothing her hand over her gray curls, Eloise smiled as she shrugged out of her jacket and hung it on a hook by the door. "There's always more than enough to do. Shall I show you the winery process today?"

Anna turned, and I could tell she was about to open her mouth to say something, but she bit her bottom lip. The moment I saw her white teeth dent the smooth pink surface, electricity sizzled down my spine. I was beginning to regret turning her down for that kiss last night.

Chapter Ten

ANNA

"Relax," Eloise said at my side.

With my hands in the gardening sink, I was rinsing off my tools. Restless to escape the pressure of being around Jasper, I'd gone out to the greenhouse to plant some fresh seedlings for flowers. I didn't really need to do this, but gardening always soothed me. Except now. It didn't seem much of anything could soothe my rattled state.

"I can't," I said as I rinsed a spade and hung it on the rack mounted on the wall beside me. "He owns half this place. And frankly, if his grandfather hadn't chosen to invest, we wouldn't be here now. There's no way Gram could've kept it afloat. I've seen the numbers myself. She lost so much money during the recession."

"I know, but he can't sell without your written permission," Eloise pointed out.

I leaned my hips against the stainless-steel sink and crossed my arms. "I know he can't, but he can tell me what to do. He owns half the business. He can make this pretty uncomfortable for me if I refuse to agree. Plus, I know he wants to sell. He wouldn't be here if he didn't."

Eloise gave me a reassuring smile. "True, but I don't think he's evil. Just a little out of his element and grumpy."

"He's used to being in charge," I muttered with a sigh.

"So what if he is?" She shrugged. "I personally think he's quite handsome," she offered with a wink.

"I'd have to be blind not to notice that." I didn't dare mention my tipsy attempt to kiss him last night. Lord knows, I'd never hear the end of it from Eloise. She was always on me to be more social and telling me I shouldn't work so hard.

I didn't have time for fun. All I ever wanted in my life was stability. My parents, God bless them, were happy-go-lucky souls who floated between a few communes when I was a little girl. Eventually, they decided I should stay full-time with my grandparents because I was falling behind in school due to the disruptions. From when I was eleven onward, I stayed with my grandmother. My grandfather passed away only a year after I moved in with them, so it was me and Gram from then on.

My parents were still around, which surprised me. They popped by occasionally, offering their haphazard love. They had a habit of asking Gram for money, which definitely hadn't helped her financial situation.

When Gram died, I'd been devastated because she was the only beacon of stability in my life. It broke my heart a little to be scrambling to straighten things out with the vineyard and flower farm she'd left me. I thought if I could just get us back on solid financial footing, I could breathe. Jasper's presence threw all of that into question.

"Hon, stop worrying so much. He's here for the month, so let him learn about the business and just see what happens. And remember, you do *not* have to sign that agreement for him to sell," Eloise said firmly.

Pushing my hips away from the sink, I let my arms drop. "I'll try. I just don't want it to be a tense situation."

"I doubt he's going to stay in California. I looked him up last night. He inherited that whole investment operation from his grandfather," Eloise said, waving her hand vaguely in the air. "He's got plenty to keep him busy back in London. I would imagine he'll just leave you in peace once he realizes you won't agree to the sale."

"Let's hope so."

Later on, Eloise graciously took Jasper all over the place with her. I wasn't sure if that's what he wanted, but she was hard to resist. She was her own force of nature, like a harsh wind where if you didn't tuck your head down, it might blow the hair off your head.

Meanwhile, I snuck upstairs to look at the accounts again. I wished I could figure out how to make the numbers work so I could just buy Jasper out. That would solve all my problems.

Unfortunately, if there was one thing I'd learned about math, it was that staring at the numbers didn't change them. Another hour later, I closed my laptop in frustration and practically stomped down the stairs. I needed to plan the menu for the wine tasting we had this week.

Eloise poked her head into where I was working downstairs with my feet hooked on the rungs of a stool at the bar with a notebook in front of me. "I'm gone for the evening," she called. "Jasper is on the loose."

For a second, I thought she meant my goat. "Oh, did he get out again?"

"No," Jasper's crisp reply came as he walked in behind Eloise through the swinging door.

"*This* Jasper," she said with a grin in his direction.

"Good night," she called, and I lifted my hand in a wave.

I wanted to invite her to stay and help me, but I didn't have the money to pay her extra. Also, I would only be asking so I wasn't stuck alone with Jasper. That would involve asking Eloise to move in, which was ridiculous.

After she left, Jasper approached, resting his palms flat on the bar across from me as he glanced down at the notebooks before bringing his gaze back to me.

Meanwhile, I was staring at his hands. He had really great hands. His hands were strong with long, almost elegant fingers. I'd discovered he was no pansy when it came to actual labor. He'd rebuilt the rickety gate into the chicken coop in the middle of the day. I hadn't even asked him, but Eloise had.

A little shiver raced through me at the thought of having him touch me. I swung my eyes up to find him watching, always watching. I instantly felt hot, heat racing over my skin and flooding my cheeks.

"How was your day?" I asked, my voice coming out squeaky.

"It was lovely."

I eyed him suspiciously. "Lovely?"

His lips twitched. "Perhaps that was overdoing it a bit. It was nice. Eloise showed me all about the wine-making process and the schedule. She also asked me to fix the gate to the chicken coop."

"I saw that. Thank you. I haven't had time to get to it," I said stiffly, hating the defensiveness that started to rise inside.

"You're handling a lot," he said, his gaze assessing me. "You could hire more help."

"I can't—" I paused, giving my head a little shake. "We can't afford it."

He was quiet for a moment before his eyes flicked down to my notebook. "What are you working on?"

"Oh, a menu for the wine tasting tomorrow. I think better when I write by hand."

"Can I see?"

"Sure." I didn't really want to show him, but I didn't feel like I had a choice. It wasn't that I had an issue with him seeing the menu, but more that I just felt plain uncomfortable about this entire situation. I turned my notebook around and slid it across the counter to him.

He lifted it, resting a hip against the bar as he turned to the side. While he was perusing it, I took the moment to absorb him. He lifted his hand, running it through his dark hair. My eyes tracked the flex of his shoulder and forearm. This man made a plain navy T-shirt look incredible. As I trailed my gaze over the corded muscles in his back, my mouth actually watered as an unsettling heat suffused me.

Why, oh why, did I have to be so attracted to *this* man? Of all men.

He set my notebook down, his intent eyes shifting back to me. "Of course, it all looks amazing. The crackers with goat cheese and orange honey sound dangerously good."

"I work with what we have here. We have bees here."

He arched a brow. "Of course, you have bees."

I felt suddenly defensive. "What do you mean, 'of course'?"

Chapter Eleven

JASPER

"I simply mean everything you make is from here. There's absolutely nothing wrong with that, Anna. I wish you wouldn't take every comment I make as a prelude to a criticism."

Anna let out a huff and pushed away from the bar, standing and curling her arms around her waist as she crossed over to the windows. Over the vineyard was an absolutely stunning sunset, casting the hillside with its rows of grapes in a pink and lavender wash.

For a beat, I felt a twinge of guilt about my comment, but for fuck's sake she needed to stop assuming I was judging everything she did.

Although, my critical voice picked up in my thoughts. *You are here to persuade her to agree to you selling. Of course, she sees you as the enemy.*

I rounded the bar, crossing over to the windows to stand beside her. "We don't have to argue for the entire month," I commented.

Anna dropped her arms, turning to face me. "You just show up in my world, telling me what to do. I'm just trying to straighten this out. Why can't you—" She let out some kind of growly sound.

"Did you just growl?"

She narrowed her eyes. "So what if I did?" As we stood there, staring at each other as if we were ready to debate, it felt as if the air filled with sparks, gathering a charge.

I wasn't even thinking when she threw her hand in the air. "You're so—" She actually growled again.

"So what?" I asked as I curled my hand around hers and stepped closer.

Okay, touching Anna was like touching a live wire. The moment we made contact, an electrical charge zigzagged through my entire body. Her cheeks went pink, and her lips parted with a startled gasp.

We stood there with our hands twined together. My thumb had landed just over her pulse on the inside of her wrist, and I could feel it humming along at a wild pace.

When Anna took a breath, I felt her breasts brush against my chest and the tight points of her nipples. Some curls had fallen loose from her ponytail and were dangling around her cheeks and neck. Her scent— earthy, sensual, and sweet— swirled around me, and it was intoxicating.

My capacity for thought had taken off like a burglar after a robbery. I wasn't thinking, not even a little, when I stepped a fraction closer and stared into her eyes. "I forgot something," I murmured.

Her mouth parted, her question coming out in a frayed whisper. "What?"

"This." Angling my head sideways, I paused for a millisecond as my lips hovered over hers. The seconds raced by and slowed to a crawl simultaneously. Sensation was moving so swiftly in my body that I couldn't stop myself. The air around us was heavy and charged, containing us in a suspended space.

The moment my lips met hers, lightning sizzled through my body. And then, I was flush against her and plundering her mouth as I slid my hand down her spine and cupped her sweet bottom. Our kiss was almost angry, both of us with our own reasons for hating our attraction to each other and the situation.

Anna kissed with abandon. Her tongue dueled with mine. She gasped into my mouth with one hand pressing into the corded muscles of my spine as I savored the feel of her soft curves. We were hard to soft, the contrast like so many other contrasts. She was all country girl, and I was a city boy. She was an American girl who loved wine and flowers, and I was a British guy who loved scotch and a rainy day in the city.

I lost all sense of time, only breaking free to lift my head and gulp in some air. It was then I realized I was rock hard with my cock nestled at the apex of her thighs. I'd cupped one of her breasts with my hand where I'd pushed the strap of her overalls out of the way and was teasing my thumb over her pebbled nipple.

Anna's round eyes met mine, hazed with passion and almost comically startled.

Chapter Twelve

ANNA

My breath was coming in sharp pants, and my pulse was skittering wildly. I stared into Jasper's eyes. I couldn't believe I'd just kissed him. More than that, I couldn't believe how much I didn't want it to stop.

I took a shuddery breath and spun away quickly, curling my arms around my waist. "Good night," I said, throwing the comment over my shoulder as I ran out of the room and up the stairs to the loft apartment.

A moment later, I sank my hips on the end of my bed and tried to get my shit together. It was just a kiss. That was it. A moment of utter insanity.

I was suddenly annoyed at what a good kisser he was. Of course, uptight, snooty

Jasper would be a good kisser. Not just good, but masterful.

Merely thinking about the feel of his palm sliding down my back and cupping my bottom sent heat spinning through me. Everything about the way that man touched me told me he had no expectation that I might not want him.

Well, you did try to kiss him the other night when you were drunk, my snide, critical voice pointed out.

Yeah, but I'm sure he's totally used to women falling at his feet.

My belly flipped over, feeling ticklish as heat bloomed over the surface of my skin again when I thought of the feel of his lips molding over mine and his tongue gliding confidently against mine.

I wasn't usually the kind of girl who melted like a warm stick of butter at nothing more than a kiss. I buried my face in my hands and took several breaths, trying to slow my pulse down.

I heard the bathroom door open and close and waited in the quiet. It wasn't even late, and here I was hiding in my bedroom because I was mortified.

A few minutes later, after hearing the toilet flush and the water run, I decided I wasn't going to hide in my room all night. I had intended to type up the menus for the wine tasting. We always did cute little things that listed the wines for the tasting and the hors d'oeuvres that paired well with them, along with suggestions for matching recipes at home.

I took a long look at myself in the mirror mounted over my dresser. My cheeks were still flushed and my lips a little swollen from his devouring kiss. God, I'd turned into a wanton girl. All over Jasper.

Smoothing my hand over my hair, I left my room. Jasper was sitting on the couch with a laptop. He'd changed out of his jeans and into a pair of sweatpants.

He looked up, his piercing gaze sweeping over me before returning to my face. I hated how comfortable he was with eye contact. I didn't even give him a second to speak and barreled ahead. "I need to work on the menus for the tasting. What are you working on?" My words came out rushed and breathy, and I silently cursed at myself.

"Dealing with email. It's never-ending."

"Oh." Striding across the room, I lifted my laptop off the desk and took it over to the kitchen counter.

As I settled in with my handwritten notes

to type, he remained quiet, yet I felt his presence the entire time I was working. I also couldn't help but think he was far more suave and experienced than I was at dealing with this whole situation. His kisses had left me feeling unsettled and all melty inside, and it was difficult to focus.

Checking my email, I ignored several from suppliers for overdue payments. I felt so helpless about the bills. I knew how to manage the winery and the flower business, and I was also pretty good with numbers, but I didn't know how to fix the pile of debt Gram had left behind.

I sensed Jasper approaching and practically every hair on my body stood with awareness. He leaned his hands on the counter at an angle across from me. "Do you usually have the same schedule every week?" he asked.

"Yeah. I've just stuck with what Gram did before. Until I can sort out the finances, it seems easiest."

He nodded. "Do you happen to know how your grandmother knew my grandfather?"

I tapped save on the last document I'd been working on and closed my laptop. "Not really. I do know she spent a semester abroad in London when she was in college. I'm assuming that might be when they met. When things got tight financially after the recession, I knew he helped out, and she made a bunch of improvements after that, like fixing up the barn where the winery is and all kinds of things. I didn't realize he owned half of the business. What do you know about them?"

Chapter Thirteen

JASPER

"About as much as you do. I suppose I have suspicions but no confirmed facts," I explained to Anna as she looked at me expectantly.

"Suspicions about what?"

She caught one of her loose curls, spinning it around her fingers. I'd been behaving myself, working quietly on the couch and relieved she had her back to me as she worked on the menus. Now, like a fool, my curiosity got the best of me after I finished plowing through my emails.

If I thought my surprising and rather inconvenient attraction to Anna was bad before, it was disastrous now that I'd kissed her.

My eyes landed on her plump pink lips, and I thought maybe I should kiss her again. Only a few feet separated us.

Hell, bloody hell, no. Be sensible. You can't seduce her into agreeing to sign off on selling your half of the business.

My angel in my brain was doing her best to slay the devil in my body. I wasn't as cold as I sensed Anna considered me. Even though I didn't know Anna well, I couldn't imagine she would take it well to feel used.

"Apparently, there's a letter waiting for me, only to be turned over after I spend a month here, according to my grandfather's barrister. My suspicions are they were in love."

"Do you think?" Her whiskey eyes went wide, and a sizzle snaked through me.

I wanted her eyes to look all hazy and surprised again. Hell, I just plain wanted her.

I kept my focus. "I do. My grandfather had a hard-core sentimental streak. I know he had a long-lost love once upon a time because he mentioned it here and there, but I never knew her name."

She stared back at me, still twirling that lock of hair. She dropped it, and her hand fell to the counter, idly tracing along the square tile edges. "Well, I suppose that would explain a lot. I never knew how they knew each other. I didn't even know his name until after she had passed away."

"Did she ever talk to you about when he became involved in the business?"

"I knew about when it happened, but not much else about it." Anna wrinkled her nose. "After my grandfather died when I was twelve, it was just Gram and me. We got by, but we weren't wealthy. During the recession, she lost a bunch of money and took out some loans to do some improvements. It was just a mess. Somewhere along the way, she seemed less stressed out and told me your grandfather had invested. She described him as an old friend, and that's it. I'm sorry you're stuck in this weird situation."

I felt a twinge of empathy for her. As annoyed as I was with the circumstances, I was getting closer and closer to keeping my half of the business. I wasn't ready to say it yet, though. If I did that, though, there was no way I couldn't get involved. It meant helping get this business back on solid financial footing. Not a single part of me was comfortable letting it float as it was.

"No need to apologize," I said, more sharply than I intended.

Anna held my gaze for a moment before nodding.

Hours later, I lay in bed wide-awake. I was awake because of an unsuspecting girl who was just a few walls away. I'd gotten up to use the loo during the night, only to see her walking through her bedroom door in nothing but a tank top and a pair of bright blue panties. I didn't think she heard me, and her back was to me. Which didn't help matters one bit because I could see her curvy, delectable bottom and her hips sway with each sleepy step.

I was irritated and annoyed and unable to slake my body's reaction to her. Giving in by early morning, I threw back the covers and went into the bathroom, taking matters into my own hands in the shower. I could imagine Anna's pink lips parting with surprise if she knew what I was doing in here with her only one room over.

———

"Theo," I said into my phone, "just send over the financials for that year."

"Which year?" my grandfather's accountant and old family friend queried.

"The year he dumped all this money into

this place. What other year would I be talking about?"

Theo chuckled. "My, my. Cranky, aren't we, this afternoon?"

"It's morning here, and I haven't had my coffee yet."

"Ah, right. You're on Pacific Standard Time. Do tell me how the weather is in California. Is it as sunny as they say?"

I chuckled. "Actually, yes. It's been sunny every single day. Lovely area. Did my grandfather ever visit here?"

"Why, yes. On two occasions. Once several decades prior, a few years after your grandmother passed away. Then he visited the year he invested. Because that's what he did, you know?"

"I'm not clear on what you mean."

"He took care of all the debts she had at the time. He didn't demand it, but she insisted on giving him half ownership. The only thing he insisted on were the guidelines about how you handled it after he passed," Theo explained.

"Do you happen to know when he put those in place?"

"When he updated his will the year before he died. He thought you were too ruthless when it came to money. He didn't want you to leave her granddaughter blowing in the wind, as he put it. I have another call coming in. Shall I email you the information?" he asked.

"Yes, please."

Ending the call, I set my phone down beside my laptop in the bedroom. Anna had been showering when I started the call, but the shower had turned off a few minutes ago. I waited until I heard her go into her bedroom before I ventured back out into the kitchen. I didn't need to accidentally encounter her half-dressed again. My libido could only take so much torture.

As soon as I heard her bedroom door close, I went out to get coffee. I was feeling irritable. I didn't particularly want to contemplate the reason, but I knew what it was. This situation was getting under my skin. I'd wanted to come out here, badger her into signing the agreement to sell, and then return to London. Now, that didn't feel right.

I wasn't particularly accustomed to being accused of having a conscience when it came to business. Oh, I was no ruthless business nightmare, but I prided myself on efficiency and making smart, strategic decisions. Nothing about holding onto half ownership of a winery and floral business drowning in debt was strategic or smart.

After a few swallows of coffee, I felt slightly better. Good timing because Anna came out of her bedroom. The second our eyes locked, that now familiar sizzle zipped through my body.

She looked fresh and lovely. The red of her hair stood out since it was damp, and her cheeks were pink. She wore a gauzy skirt with a T-shirt. And, bloody hell, why couldn't she wear baggy T-shirts? Today her T-shirt was another V-neck that hugged her breasts with a row of tiny buttons. My eyes dipped immediately down to the lush curves out-lining the V between her breasts.

My early morning attempt to relieve my seemingly endless desire for her turned out to be fleeting. I took a breath. "Good morning, Anna."

She looked at me for a second before crossing the room silently to get a cup of coffee. Only after she filled her mug and took a swallow did she look over at me again where I stood beside the kitchen island.

"I couldn't help but overhear your call this morning. Why don't you just ask me for the paperwork? I'm sure I can find it," she said sharply, defensiveness and sheer contrariness coming off her in waves.

Damn. This woman knew how to get under my skin. As she stared at me, her eyes narrowed and her lips pursed.

"I was wondering what my grandfather had on record. I'm just trying to sort out what the financial situation is here and how my grandfather came to own half of the business."

"What did you find out?"

"The timing and that your grandmother was the one who insisted he own half the business when he loaned her the money to help and paid off the debts she had at the time."

Anna looked dismayed. "And? If he paid off her debts, why is there so much now?"

Good Lord. I thought she was about to cry. I felt that uncomfortable twinge. Again.

"I can't answer the questions about your grandmother's decisions, but perhaps you can. Did she use an accountant or an attorney?"

She took a gulp of her coffee, straightening her shoulders slightly. "No. She did everything herself. Even before things got all screwed up. Look, I know how to make wine and handle the flowers and do all those things. I'm excellent at math, but I'm not an accountant, and it seems she tangled every-thing up. I don't want to ask for help, but I need it. Maybe you can help me figure out exactly how bad things are."

Chapter Fourteen

ANNA

My heart was pounding in an unsteady beat—a combination of my body's near constant reaction to Jasper, which was only getting worse with every passing day that he was here, and anxiety about asking for help.

My rather flighty early childhood had left me craving only two things—stability and the ability to control my own circumstances. My grandmother had represented that for me after I finally got to stay with her when my parents moved on to travel for a few years. It hurt to feel a little angry with her for leaving me the business in such bad shape without telling me.

I'd known things weren't great after the recession. They weren't for anyone, but here we were now, years later after that, and I was trying to pull everything together. I was afraid I wasn't going to succeed. I hated, absolutely hated, not being able to figure it all out myself. I was sure I could. But the one thing I couldn't conjure up was more time, and that was in desperately short supply.

Jasper was quiet, long enough that I began to berate myself for even asking, but then he dipped his chin in acknowledgment. "Of course, I'll help. No matter what happens, we own this place together. Maybe we didn't plan it that way, but it's the situation in which we find ourselves."

My relief was so immense I didn't even hide my shuddering sigh. "Thank you."

"What other records did your grandmother leave behind?"

"Do you mean aside from her spreadsheets?" At his nod, I looked across the room and gestured to the file cabinet. "Those."

Jasper eyed the innocuous beige file cabinet, looking thoughtful. "That's it?" he asked as his eyes swung back to me.

"That I know of. Before she updated this building, she used to keep everything out at their house."

"And where is that?"

"Just down the street." Jasper looked confused, so I explained, "She did a reverse mortgage, so she owed a bunch of money. Right now, the house is just sitting there. She had enough sense not to leave it to me because then I would be stuck with the reverse mortgage. I don't know what's going on with the bank, but the house is empty."

"Have you been in there?" he pressed.

I chewed on my bottom lip before shaking my head. "No. Technically, it's not mine, so I didn't think it was smart to go in there."

"I will," he said flatly in his snooty British accent. "We might as well see what else she left behind. I know enough to know the finances aren't looking good, but we might as well be working with a full hand."

"Hand?"

"A hand of cards. From what I've seen, she only has the past five years in her spreadsheets. I would like to see what else there is." He paused, looking at me carefully. "If you don't mind me asking, did your grandmother experience any cognitive decline?"

My throat felt tight. I knew he might eventually wonder about that. "Yes. That's what has me worried. Things could be even worse than I know."

Jasper nodded slowly. "Maybe not. Maybe

she lost track of some things that would make the situation better."

"How do you propose we get into the house?"

"When's the last time you were in the house?"

"About five years ago. That was after your grandfather got involved. She had the money to fix things up here. When the bank moved to foreclose on her home, she just moved out. I'd been away in college and came home then. I'm guessing she chose not to tell your grandfather about the mortgage problems."

"I say we just drive down there."

I opened my mouth to argue, but there was no reason not to try.

"Okay. I need to do the morning feeding, but then we can go."

"Shall I help?"

I held his gaze and shrugged. "It's up to you. I appreciate the offer, but I certainly don't expect it."

Jasper's lips curled in a slight smile, and my belly flipped. "I'm not particularly good at staying idle. I never did see myself working on a farm like this, but I don't mind helping with the goats and the chickens."

———

I stared at the yellow tape with Do Not Enter labeled on it and felt a little nervous. Stopping at the door, I scanned the letter taped there. The paper was wrinkled and the print slightly faded, but the covered porch had kept it dry for the most part.

Property of bank. Do not enter without permission.

"Are you sure we should just go in?" I asked as Jasper came around from the back of the house.

"Yes. You have a key. Let's use it," he said confidently.

A minute later, we stepped inside the home where I'd spent the most stable years of my childhood. The space had a unique quality of stillness, the feeling that no one had been here in too long. The curtains were closed, save for those over one window.

A shaft of sunlight came through that window, illuminating the dust moats floating in the air, stirred up from our entrance. A sense of nostalgia slammed into me. There was a table in the corner where I did my homework in middle and high school, and the old floral couch with its ruffle against the wall under the window facing the street.

Gram's house was small. The front area was just a living room with an archway that led into a dining room. The kitchen was through another archway directly on the other side of the dining room. A short hallway led to two bedrooms and a bathroom.

I felt Jasper's eyes on me. "You okay?" he asked.

I swallowed and nodded. "Yeah."

He seemed to be waiting for me, so I gave myself a mental shake and strode into the dining room. "This is where she kept her files." The dining room was more the office than an actual dining room although we did eat in this room when I lived here. "Oh, they're all here!" I was surprised to see four file cabinets set against the wall.

Jasper was right behind me and stopped in front of the file cabinets as I pushed the curtains open so we could see better. "Surprised?" he asked.

"I guess I thought she would've taken these," I replied slowly.

"When did the bank initiate foreclosure proceedings?"

"While I was away in college, so I'm not exactly sure of the date."

He nodded, his eyes scanning the file cabinets. "Often, people think situations like that will resolve themselves. Maybe she thought it would, and she would have time to come back."

"Oh, she definitely thought that," I said with a painful beat of my heart. She'd been so let down by the entire situation and scrambled to make things work when she moved into the upstairs of the winery.

"Can I open the file cabinets?"

"Of course. That's what we're here for, right?"

"Well, yes, but this is your grandmother's home."

I was feeling strange—emotional and numb at the same time. "Not anymore," I said quickly. "I'd like to just move the file cabinets, but I imagine that's a bit of work."

When I looked back at Jasper, I felt as if he was trying to assess how I was doing. I didn't want him to think I was an emotional mess. Restless, I crossed the room and opened the top file drawer, only to find it was chock-full of paperwork.

Of course, that was to be expected. But suddenly, I was blinking back tears—over a filing cabinet and paperwork. I swallowed through the tight feeling in my throat and chest. I heard Jasper's footsteps retreating from the room and wasn't sure if I was relieved or annoyed.

My eyes scanned the labels written in my grandmother's tidy penmanship—labeled by year and what appeared to be companies and accounts. A moment later, Jasper reappeared with plastic crates in hand.

"Where did you find those?" I asked.

"I saw them around back. There's enough for everything in these filing cabinets."

I wanted to burst into tears all over again, but I didn't. Inside of roughly half an hour, Jasper had efficiently emptied the papers in the filing cabinets into the plastic crates and carried them out to the car.

We worked mostly in silence, for which I was relieved. I didn't have it in me to talk, not while I was dealing with this avalanche of emotion. I was also unaccountably distracted by his presence even though I was starting to discover that was the case almost all the time.

I did a quick loop through the old house to see if Gram had left anything else behind, then we drove back to the vineyard. Other than the furnishings and a bottle of aspirin with a single aspirin in the medicine cabinet, there was nothing else personal here.

I followed Jasper into the winery, my eyes watching the flex of his shoulders as he carried crates. For a businessman, he was in awfully good shape.

It was only after we got everything put away and had the crates lined up in a row underneath the windows upstairs that I abruptly lost control. I was leaning over, curiously reading my name on one of the faded manila file folders. When I pulled it out and opened it, I found one of my pictures from school. All of the sudden, tears were rolling down my cheeks.

Jasper had gone downstairs and returned. I was swiping the tears off my cheeks when I heard him approaching. "Anna?"

"Yeah?" I asked.

He stopped beside me. When I turned and saw a glimmer of understanding in his eyes, I was crying all over again. I didn't really understand how it happened, but the next thing I knew, I was sobbing against his delectable chest as he held me wordlessly, and his palm moved up and down my back in a soothing caress.

Somehow, going into my grandmother's old home set off an emotional storm inside. I felt as if I'd been holding myself together for too long now. First, it was the stress and grief of facing her death. Initially, I didn't grasp the shaky financial situation of the business and simply threw myself into work. It was only about six months or so ago that I became fully aware of just what a mess I was facing. I had tried to march forward, telling myself over and over it would somehow work itself out.

Then I heard about Jasper's grandfather passing away and had tried to push my tendency to fret about what might happen next to the back of my mind. Until Jasper showed up, yanking the rug out from under my feet.

Tangling inside all of this was my inconvenient and confusing desire for him. I couldn't even believe I was turning to him for comfort. It wasn't as if I thought about it. He was just there, and I reflexively sought his support.

After a few moments, I caught my breath, and the jumble of emotion started to pass. Of course, as soon as my emotions took a back seat, desire jumped to the forefront and grabbed the steering wheel. Jasper smelled good. Like sunshine, if sunshine had a smell. I didn't know what laundry soap he used, but it was yummy.

My heart started to pound, and heat sparked inside me, scattering everywhere and sending a prickle down my spine. I stood there, trying to collect myself and mentally ordering myself to step back, but I couldn't seem to do it. Not with his muscled chest pressing against me. My nipples tightened to an ache.

Jasper's hand stilled on my back, and I heard his heartbeat, rapid and steady, under my ear. I thought maybe I was crazy, but then I felt the presence of his arousal, hard and hot against my hip. I tried to take a breath, only succeeding in getting a shallow sip of air.

I finally lifted my head. When my eyes ran into his, I felt caught. His eyes were dark and unreadable.

I started to step back, but he held me fast. "Tell me, Anna, what do you want?"

The intoxicating timbre of his voice was low and taut with that crisp, deliciously commanding tone.

Chapter Fifteen

JASPER

I'd lost my mind. This entire day had gone skidding sideways. Now, I found myself with the utterly delectable Anna in my arms. Her brown eyes were wide as she stared up at me.

For God's sake, she'd just been crying. And me, the one who avoided emotion and drama at all costs, had comforted her. Now, at a most inconvenient moment, my body was on fire, humming with need for her. So hot, it was like water dropped on a hot pan when it sizzled and steam rose through the air.

Anna's cheeks were pink, and I could feel her nipples pressing through the layers of fabric between us. My mouth practically watered at the thought of baring one of her lovely, round breasts and sucking her nipple into my mouth.

Her pink tongue darted out and swiped the corner of her mouth. She was breathing in these short pants while my heartbeat pounded an echo through my body. One of her hands was curled into a fist between us. It slowly opened until it was pressed flat on my chest just over my heartbeat. My cock was heavy, and I knew she could feel it.

She finally answered my question. "To kiss you."

Now, see, that was what made me really lose my mind. Anna was supposed to be a good girl and tell me to get the hell away from her because I wasn't the man for her. She was all sunshine and flowers and sweet. I tended to be cranky, and I treated everything, including women, like business. I had absolutely *no* business wanting to kiss this girl, but I wanted it more than I wanted my next breath of air. And air was in short supply here.

What I should've done didn't really matter because the moment Anna rasped her soft request, my eyes traced her face. Starting at the arch of her brows, my gaze lingered for a moment on her whiskey gaze before glancing over the charming smatter of freckles on her cheeks, so light as to be barely there. My eyes finally landed on her full and pink lips with that barely there dimple in the center of her bottom lip.

My hand moved on its own. There didn't seem to be much thought in anything I did when it came to Anna. Case in point: I was here on business. Specifically, to get rid of my stake in this business with her. The layers of complications I was creating by kissing her again couldn't be overstated. My rational brain knew perfectly well I was being stupid, yet I didn't give a damn.

When I lifted my eyes to hers again, our gazes stayed locked together. My nerve endings felt as if they were on fire, sizzling from the sheer electric power of being near her. Dipping my head, I moved slowly, almost wondering if she was going to come to her senses. Maybe one of us could be sensible.

I was relieved when she didn't. Instead, I felt the press of her fingers right over the taut muscles at the base of my spine as she leaned up and pressed her lips to the divot at the base of my throat. That kiss was brief, but fire licked over my skin from the point of contact. Then my hand was sliding into her silky soft hair as I dipped my head.

For a millisecond, the kiss was gentle, but

then it turned into an inferno. Or perhaps, it was me who turned into an inferno. Because Anna made me flat-out crazy. I wanted her with a ferocity that startled me with its intensity.

The second her tongue glided against mine, I angled her head to the side and devoured her mouth. Diving into the warm sweetness, she tasted a little minty. Her tongue was sassy, twining against mine as she sighed into my mouth and flexed against me.

By some miracle, she wasn't wearing overalls today. My hand slid down her back, gratified at how I could feel the heat of her skin through the thin cotton of her skirt. When my palm smoothed over the curve of her hip, the soft give of her flesh under my touch had me growling against her lips.

Our tongues tangled, and I felt the score of her nails on my back through the cotton before her hand stole under my shirt. When her palm slid over my skin, it felt as if sparks were landing on me. Everywhere she touched me was a fire burning and feeding an almost unbearable need for more.

In keeping with the not-thinking theme, I didn't even know how I got over to the couch, but the next thing I knew, I was pulling her onto my lap, murmuring, "Fuck me, Anna girl. You're too hot for words." I was out of my mind with lust.

Later, I would have to ponder the fact I was speaking at all. I wasn't much for being chatty when it came to sex. I was all about efficient achievement of pleasure.

There was plenty of pleasure with Anna's soft curves in my lap and her skirt riding up around her thighs. Efficiency was the furthest thing from my mind. It was a surfeit of pleasure with the silky skin of her thighs causing me to nip the side of her neck, growling and chuckling when she let out a little squeak.

"I need to see that chest," she muttered in a bossy tone as she shoved at my shirt.

Though I was reluctant to take my hands off her body, I reached behind my neck to yank my shirt up and over my head, but then I quickly set to work on the tiny buttons on her shirt. "I need to see you too," I murmured against her throat as I pressed a hot kiss there.

Anna let out a breathy sigh when her shirt fell open. I was struck silent for a moment. She was wearing a sheer cream lace bra, and the dusky pink of her nipples was visible through the lace. Impatient, I flicked the clasp open between her breasts.

My cock swelled when her plump breasts

tumbled free. I cupped one with my hand, savoring the lush weight as I dipped my head and sucked her nipple. I needed her, needed everything.

Her fingers speared in my hair, and she shifted on my lap. I could feel her hot core rocking over the hard length of my arousal. I felt out of control in a way I'd never felt. Sensations were threatening to trample what little common sense I had left.

I lifted my head, leaning back. Opening my eyes, I took Anna in. There she sat with her shirt falling open. Her skin was flushed, and her chest rose and fell rapidly with each raspy breath. She was so fucking sexy I could barely stand it.

I wanted to bury myself in this sweet, sassy country girl whose business was careening toward disaster and whose heart was breaking because of it. Lifting a hand, I trailed my fingertip along her jaw, down the side of her neck, and over the sweet curve of one of her breasts before I rolled her nipple between my thumb and forefinger.

She was so responsive. Her lips parted, and she let out a low moan. My hand coasted over the soft curve of her belly to the apex between her thighs. With her skirt riding up, I glimpsed blue cotton panties. She was a practical kind of girl, which made her even more mind-bendingly sexy.

Straightening, she bit her lip as she stared at me. Her eyes were so dark they were almost black. I watched her as I teased my knuckles over the swollen nub I could feel through the cotton.

"Tell me what else you want," I murmured. "I've already kissed you."

"More," she demanded.

When I pushed the cotton out of the way and my fingers were coated with the slick juices of her arousal, I could feel the tines of my zipper pressing against my cock. I might've been half out of mind with lust for her, but I was only going to take this so far today. Perhaps I was torturing myself, or perhaps it was some misguided idea to think I had some control.

It didn't matter. I sank two fingers in her channel, watching as her eyes closed and she rocked into my touch. It was a slow tease as I fucked her with my fingers and watched this girl with absolutely no artifice drive me all the way to the edge of my control, so far it was almost frightening.

I wanted nothing more than *her* pleasure. So fiercely, it almost hurt.

She whimpered, "Jasper."

Her breasts jutted out. I leaned forward to catch a nipple with my mouth as I pumped once again with my fingers and lightly teased my thumb over her clit.

"Come on," I encouraged, speaking against her skin. "Give it to me."

Her next cry was ragged, and her channel rippled around my fingers as she came with a noisy shudder.

Anna fell against me, her forehead pressing against the side of my neck. I could feel the heated gusts of her breath over my skin. I scrambled for control, anything to convince myself I wasn't completely lost to this woman and to this force of desire that was unlike anything in my experience. I was a slave to it. I knew it wasn't over, not even close.

After a moment, she lifted her head, and I opened my eyes. Her hazy gaze coasted over my face. Still scrambling for purchase, I grasped onto the one thing that'd served me well in all moments of uncertainty—set the tone, dictate the pace. "Now, we have work to do," I said.

Chapter Sixteen

ANNA

Now, we have work to do.

"Way to make a girl feel special," I muttered to myself as Jasper's words played in my mind from last night.

I carefully set a spray of hyacinth to surround the daisies nestled in the center of the vase. Stepping back, I smiled to myself. My very favorite flowers were the simplest. My grandmother had prided herself on growing and selling flowers that were easy and common as a way to remind the world that beauty was approachable.

Of course, Jasper *had* made me feel rather special by giving me an absolutely glorious orgasm. The man truly had magic fingers and lips and teeth and tongue and just, well, everything. God, he was delicious. His chest? A fucking work of art. All warm muscled planes with just a dusting of hair.

After that melting and mind-blowing encounter, we had, in fact, gotten to work. Jasper was like a machine the second he had papers in front of him. His studious concentration was even sexy. His focus. Who thought focus was sexy?

Me, apparently. It helped that the package wrapped around all that focus was this weird combination of distinguished British gentleman wrapped in a muscled, lean body paired with a dirty mouth. God, the things he whispered when I was about to come made me blush all over again just now. It wasn't so much the words, but the tone behind them.

A part of me felt a little salty about how quickly he'd shifted gears, but it had saved me from myself. Being busy kept me from doing or saying anything stupid. After my little emotional outburst and transition into writhing on his lap, well, I needed to not do anything else ridiculous.

We had a wine tasting tonight, and I only had two hours to finish getting ready. Gathering several flower arrangements together, I put them in a tray and hurried from the greenhouse over to the winery. Jasper, the goat, who I now had to refer to as "the goat" every time I saw him, came trotting across the yard. He gave a little buck with his feet and then bumped his head into my knees.

"Hey, sweetie." I tried to rub his chin with my knee since my hands were full. "Eloise is going to feed you tonight," I said conversationally as I kept walking with him meandering along beside me. In another moment, he was distracted and veered over when he saw Tinker Bell munching on some lettuce.

I'd learned from Gram how important it was to simply plant things for the sole purpose of the goats eating them. Otherwise, they destroyed everything you had. The latest goats we had weren't the first, but Jasper and Tinker Bell loved what most goats loved. They would eat anything and everything, so they needed things to keep them happy. They loved lettuce, so we planted lettuce for them every year.

Using my shoulder, I pushed through the back door into the kitchen. Eloise was bustling around and brushed the back of her wrist over her forehead to push a lock of curly gray hair out of her eyes.

"Hey, girl," she called. "I think we're just

about ready. If you want to do your magic out front, I'll take care of the animals before I clock out for tonight. Do you have anyone helping you tonight?"

I set the tray on the counter and gave my hands a shake. "No. Jasper said he wanted to help, and I figured that would be enough. Have you seen him?"

"Just a bit ago. He's awfully easy on the eyes, don't you think?"

Eloise just wouldn't quit with trying to get a rise out of me about Jasper. "I have eyes," I quipped in return, turning away and hoping she didn't notice the flush I felt creeping up my cheeks.

"He's got eyes too," she said. "They're usually stuck on you."

My head whipped around so fast, I was surprised I didn't give myself whiplash.

Eloise grinned. "I knew it. You *do* think he's cute, don't you?"

"Of course, I do. I can't do anything about it."

My mind whispered, *"You already kissed him, and just last night, he had his fingers buried inside of you while you came all over them."*

I could ignore that stupidity.

"It seems he's trying to help, and I hope

you're letting him," she said, her eyes sobering.

"He's trying to make sure I'll agree to let him sell his half." Worry struck me so hard it felt as if I was choking. This kind of anxiety was like a whirling dervish in my chest, and it scared me.

"Hon, you have been carrying this all by yourself since your Gram died. It's a lot of work. Even if he wants to sell, it's not gonna do any harm to have his help cleaning up the financial mess. You never talk about it, but you and I both know your grandma was not totally sharp during her last few years. You can still love her and acknowledge that," she said, her tone soothing.

My shoulders sagged, and I turned and leaned my hips against the counter. I curled my hands around the edge, and the cool surface slightly settled me. "I know. I don't like to talk about it because there's nothing I can do about it."

Eloise stopped in front of me, her eyes sympathetic. "You have done an incredible job with the flowers and the winery. In fact, you're running it tighter than your grandmother ever did at her best. Organization was never her strong suit. You are magic with the flowers.

You're going to keep winning awards for the wines here, and no one is going to forget that. Let Jasper help you with the finances. It's not about brains, hon. Just about having the patience and the time to plow through all the old stuff your grandmother left behind."

I chewed on the inside of my cheek as I eyed her. "I know. I'm letting him. I've given him free rein of everything. I just hope he doesn't use what he finds to screw me over. He's not exactly warm and fuzzy."

The moment I spoke, I felt a twinge of guilt for that comment. Grumpy, sexy qualities aside, when I'd burst into tears yesterday, Jasper had comforted me. He wasn't an asshole, and I knew it.

As if she could read my mind, Eloise said, "He's not an asshole. He's just a sexy kind of uptight British businessman. You do your thing and let him do his. It just might work out. Now, I gotta go." She looked out the kitchen window. "Oh God, Jasper and Tinker Bell are headed over to the flowers."

Eloise was off, dust kicking out from her shoes as she raced out the door with me right behind her.

———

"Damn, this is a good wine," Chance said in his usual magnanimous and enthusiastic fashion.

Aubrey caught my eye and smiled. Chance had one arm around her waist and a glass of our latest award-winning wine in his other hand. It was one of the sweet reds, my personal favorite type of wine.

The wine tasting was crowded with people bustling all around. Jasper had turned out to be more helpful than expected. He stayed on top of serving wine, and I handled the orders. He might not have done much customer service before, but his charming smile and British accent had the ladies flocking over to him. We'd already beat our record for sales in a single evening.

Aubrey cast a teasing glance toward Jasper. He was currently in the middle of a conversation with three women. They appeared to be vying for his attention while he appeared coolly unaffected. "Jasper's the toast of the evening," she commented.

"If it sells wine, it works for me," I replied, entirely truthfully. "I hope Pixy is enjoying his playdate," I offered to Chance when I noticed him looking out the back window toward where Pixy was currently frolicking with Tinker Bell and Jasper.

Chance grinned. "Of course, he is. At home, he just has humans. You should run a goat daycare," he suggested.

Aubrey burst out laughing. "Babe, that's ridiculous."

At that moment, Jasper, remarkably free from female attention, paused beside us. "Need any refills?" His eyes scanned our glasses.

"I'll take one," I replied.

"I think we're all set," Aubrey said. "We need to get going soon."

"Hey, what do you think of a goat daycare?" Chance asked Jasper.

To Jasper's credit, his lips barely twitched as his alert gaze flicked from Chance to me. "I suppose that could be an interesting business venture if there were enough pet goats who needed daycare," he offered in his crisp tone.

Chance nodded thoughtfully. "I suppose. Pixy loves coming to see Jasper and Tinker Bell."

Another woman approached Jasper, and he lifted his finger, letting me know he'd be back with a fresh glass of wine for me. I didn't need to be waited on, though, so I made my way over to the bar myself, sliding behind it and refilling my glass while also helping a few customers.

The night passed quickly, as did every night when we had a wine-tasting event. I enjoyed a bit more of our latest batch of wine than usual. I vaguely recalled Jasper steadying me when I stumbled as I climbed upstairs to go to bed. I didn't remember anything else, so I was surprised when I woke during the night to find myself in a T-shirt and underwear and tucked in my bed.

My head was already working up to a rager of a headache, and my bladder was nagging me about my need to get out of bed even though I didn't want to. Rolling my head to the side, I saw that the digital clock on the table beside my bed read 3:07 a.m. There was no sense in trying to sleep through until morning without going to the bathroom.

I groaned and put my hands to my forehead when I sat up. I knew I'd had a little too much to drink last night. Jasper kept my nerves unsettled, yet I couldn't really blame him. It was my response to him, and I just couldn't seem to get it under control.

Moving gingerly, I tiptoed out of my bedroom and took care of business in the bathroom. When I flicked on the light to search for some ibuprofen, I was surprised to see a glass of water with two ibuprofen tablets sitting on the counter with a note beside it.

I predict you'll have a headache. This is for when you get up. —J

Did he have to be so thoughtful? It was hard to reconcile his cool, polite manner with a man who had pretty much blown my mind and dragged my body into meltdown territory, only to end it all by saying, "Now, we have work to do."

I was no dummy, so I took the ibuprofen and finished the glass of water before making my way back to bed, hoping I didn't say anything stupid last night.

When I woke two hours later—my body familiar with what time I usually got up despite my potential hangover—I was surprised to discover my clothes neatly folded and laid on the chair on top of my dresser. My cheeks got hot because I wondered if Jasper had undressed me. Dear God. I needed to remember not to let myself enjoy any of my favorite wines while he was here.

Chapter Seventeen

JASPER

I studiously tried not to notice the way the sun glinted on Anna's strawberry blond hair. She was outside doing something in the flower field. I tried even harder not to notice how cute she looked in her overalls. Apparently, I had a bit of a *thing* for overalls. Well, a thing for me as long as Anna was wearing them. I wanted her to wear them every day, preferably with one of her cute little tank tops.

I looked back down at the desk. I had devised a system for getting through the haphazardly organized files from Anna's grandmother, so I didn't have much left. While I'd discovered no miracles yet, I had filled in some of the blanks. Eloise had also confirmed that Anna's grandmother had definitely not been at her sharpest the last few years. From what I could piece together, she'd been behind with personal bills in addition to the business. Whether it was pride or something else, she didn't use any of the money from my grandfather to help with her personal bills. It snowballed over time, so she'd started taking out more and more from the business to try to save the house. In the end, it all left Anna in a messy situation when her grandmother died.

When my phone rang, and I looked down to see my solicitor's phone number on the screen, I answered immediately. "Hello."

"Jasper, thought I would check in and see how things are going in California. Any thoughts about your plans?" Benjamin asked.

I opened my mouth to tell him that, of course, I still intended to persuade Anna to agree to let me sell, but then I hesitated. That hesitation revealed more than I wanted to contemplate about myself. "I'm still getting up to speed on everything, and I've got a full three weeks left here."

"Ah, I see. All right, then. Please do keep me informed so I can make sure to prepare any paperwork necessary in a timely manner."

"Absolutely. I'm curious about something."

"I'm not sure if I can help, but what is it?"

"What do you know about the nature of my grandfather's relationship with Hannah Lennon?"

There was a beat of silence before he replied, "Simply that he knew her for many years. He considered her a friend. She did not ask for his assistance, by the way. He had me checking in on things. When he learned she was struggling and looking into selling the winery, he intervened immediately."

"Hmm. That's all you know?" I prompted.

"That's it. I thought you should know Anna Lennon emailed me to confirm the details related to the will and the business. I confirmed them for her."

That didn't surprise me. "Ah, I see. I'd imagine she would. It's not a typical arrangement."

"No, it's not," he agreed. "Is there anything else I can help with?"

"Not at the moment, but thank you. I'll reach out as soon as I know my plans."

After I ended the call, I leaned back in my chair and ran a hand through my hair. I'd thought I would come to California and discover that my co-owner was just as anxious to be rid of me as I was to be rid of the business. I'd expected to discover my co-owner wanted to sweep my inconvenient appearance out of her life. I hadn't even figured on even staying out the month.

In all honesty, I hadn't counted on any of this. My worst-case scenario involved me staying here—as required by the terms of my grandfather's will—and biding my time.

I certainly hadn't expected to arrive and get knocked off balance by a girl whose penchant for overalls was ruining me by the day. I definitely hadn't counted on finding myself wanting to dig into the finances and straighten out the mess left behind by her grandmother. I absolutely hadn't counted on wanting Anna. Bloody hell, the girl had set up house inside my brain. I didn't think I could evict her.

Every effort I made at trying to gain control of the situation felt like trying to catch dust in the air. Every motion only chased my control further away.

Two days had passed since I lost my mind and watched Anna fly apart on my lap. She was making me feel half crazy. I was clearly going bonkers. For her.

Case in point: the other night after the wine tasting. She was tipsy, very tipsy. She tried to kiss me. Again. I'd never in my life considered myself the virtuous one when it came to women making passes at me, yet there I was, being virtuous.

I'd carefully set her back, ignoring how sexy she looked when she actually pouted. I'd even had to walk her upstairs and get her into bed. The temptation of Anna yanking her clothes off in front of me and revealing the freckles scattered like stardust on her skin was a temptation beyond all reason. I hadn't given in. Oh, no. As I said, I was virtuous.

I found a T-shirt in the top drawer of her dresser and carefully covered up her gorgeous, plump, and bouncy breasts and then tucked her under the covers. Blessedly, she'd started snoring within seconds.

Shaking my thoughts off *that* hot vision, I leaned forward, resting my chin in my hand. Anna had let me move the desk, so it offered the wide view of the fields. I hadn't been thinking of her when I asked about that, but at that moment, she was front and center in my view. She wore a woven straw hat to shade the bright sunshine with her strawberry curls escaping. It was a whimsical touch to go with her overalls and purple polka-dotted rubber boots with a matching purple tank top.

Even from this distance, I felt the buzz of

desire fizzing in my veins. When she was physically close, the air felt filled with sparks, all of them colliding together and creating more energy. At some point, I would lose control, and there would be an explosion.

I forced my attention away from her and dug back into the files. Only moments later, I stumbled across a major find. Restless, I stood from the desk, contemplating when I should tell Anna what I discovered.

Her grandmother had apparently forgotten about an investment account set up by her husband who passed away years before she did. It was chock-full of money. If she'd hired a forensic accountant after her grandmother died, they might've found this. As it was, that happened to be my specialty.

It spoke volumes that I hesitated to tell her. With this money, she could buy me out. Then I would have an excuse to leave sooner.

"Fuck," I muttered to myself.

When I stepped into the guest bedroom, I laughed when I caught a glimpse of myself in the mirror. Out of pure habit, I'd dressed as if I were working today. I wasn't wearing a suit, but I had put on a button-down shirt and a pair of slacks. It was ridiculous, really.

I changed quickly into jeans and a faded navy-blue T-shirt. Then I made my way downstairs. When I poked my head into the back room where the magic wine making happened, I found Eloise hard at work. She was putting new bottles of wine in a rack. They had a system that organized the wine by type and year. It was meticulously organized, in contrast to the financial records.

Eloise straightened, casting me a wide smile as she approached. "Well, hello there, Jasper. What brings you down here this afternoon?"

"Just checking on things. Do you happen to know what Anna's working on today?"

Eloise studied me for a moment, and I didn't miss the subtle, knowing glint contained in her gaze. "The flowers. When she's stressed, that's what she does. It helps that there's always something to do, even if it's just weeding. She also said she was going to get some honey from the beehives."

"Pardon me?"

Eloise grinned. "Honey. From the beehives. Don't worry, she'll put on her bee outfit."

"Where are the bees?"

Eloise waved vaguely toward the flower fields. "Out toward the back. She keeps flowers that bees love planted near their hives so they stay happy."

"Interesting."

"You seem to find Anna quite interesting," she offered with another grin.

I elected to ignore that observation. "Good day, Eloise." I nodded and then strode outside, intending to find Anna and see just what getting honey from the bees entailed.

Chapter Eighteen

ANNA

"Hey there," I murmured as I reached into the beehive. "Are you taking good care of your queen?"

Of course, I had absolutely *no* freaking clue if the bees were listening to me. Much less if they understood the English language. Rather arrogant of us humans to think insects and other creatures could speak our language. That said, I hoped they could sense my intent, which was to do no harm.

My vision wasn't too great through the clear plastic section over my face since I wore the bee suit. Peering inside, I carefully removed the honey frame. This hive was my healthiest hive yet. It had now survived two winters.

I placed the frame in a wheelbarrow where I also had some plants to take to the greenhouse. I checked on a few other things for the hive and then stepped back. The bees buzzed around me but dispersed as I moved away from the hive with the wheelbarrow. I pushed back the hood on my bee suit. As soon as I turned around, I discovered Jasper only about ten feet away. His eyes were laughing.

I felt myself blushing. I generally felt like a country bumpkin around him, and now I was in my bee suit, which was the very opposite of sexy. Somehow, even in jeans and a T-shirt, he exuded a cool elegance.

"Just getting some honey." I wiggled the wheelbarrow as if I needed proof of why I was wearing my shapeless bee suit.

"So I gathered," he replied. "Any problems?"

"Not at all."

"Do you always talk to the bees?" he asked, his lips quirking.

I rolled my eyes, attempting to shrug nonchalantly. "Yes. I want to make sure they're calm and know that I mean them no harm."

He nodded slowly. "Good point." He fell into stride beside me as I began to walk through the rows of flowers. "Is there anything you don't grow or cultivate here?"

"There are lots of things we don't grow here."

"Not that I can see. You grow your own vegetables, herbs, and flowers. You make your own wine, and you have goats for making your own fresh cheese. You even have chickens for fresh eggs, and you have beehives."

"We don't slaughter meat here," I offered.

Jasper's low chuckle sent a prickle of heat chasing down my spine and scattering like sparks through the rest of my body. "I don't suppose you do. Is that a business venture we should take on?"

"We?"

His pace slowed before he resumed. "Yes, we. I mean, *we* do own this business together."

He couldn't know that every time he said "we," I thought of myself straddling him on the couch, half-naked with his fingers buried inside me. Unsettled, I snapped, "Don't make light of it. Unless you're going to stay on and not badger me into agreeing to let you sell, don't pretend we're partners."

My voice was sharp, and I felt a twinge of guilt as soon as I spoke. Jasper fell quiet for several seconds before replying, "I understand your frustration, Anna." He stopped and turned to look at me.

I wanted to storm past him, but that was childish, and I considered myself an adult, both in age and behavior. Feeling frumpy, I turned to face him. "Do you, really? I don't know if you do. This is all I know, and I don't know what I'll do if you insist on selling. I'm not exactly in a position to make this work on my own. And—" My words screeched to a halt as a rush of tears threatened, wicking from the tight knot in my throat and stinging hot in my eyes.

Shaking my head swiftly, I turned and practically ran the rest of the way back to the winery kitchen. I prayed Jasper had enough sense to leave me be, at least for now. It wasn't as if I could escape forever.

Chapter Nineteen

JASPER

For a split second, I almost broke into a jog to race after Anna, but then I held myself back, solely because I knew she wanted to be left alone. I was turning into a sensitive fool, worrying about her feelings. This was a business situation, and I needed to make a business decision.

When I stepped into the winery kitchen a few minutes later, there was no sign of Anna. Eloise was washing her hands in the sink and glanced over.

"What happened?" she asked.

"I used my superpower," I said dryly.

"What would that be?" she countered.

"Annoying Anna."

Eloise cast me a sympathetic smile. "I'm

sure it will be fine. She's usually pretty easy-going. It's been a hard year for her since her grandma passed, and she's been trying to straighten things out. She has no one, except her friends."

"Where are her parents, if you don't mind me asking?"

Eloise turned off the faucet and shook the water from her hands before drying them. After hanging up the towel, she leaned her hips against the sink and let out a sigh. "Who knows? Certainly not me. Two total flakes, if you're asking my opinion."

"Can you clarify?"

"Does Britain have hippies?'

"Sure, I think."

"Actually, that's not fair. Most people would describe me as an aging hippy. I was all about peace and love back in the 60s and 70s. However, once I had a daughter, I lived a stable life and made sure she was taken care of. Anna's parents drifted around. For a while, they lived at a commune about an hour away from here. Half the time they were gone, leaving Anna in the care of whatever teenager happened to be available for free babysitting—skill set not important. That girl craved stability and was so relieved when she finally got to stay here with her grandparents. So yeah, it's been hard. First, her grandfather died not long after she started to stay with them, and then her grandma last year. And bless her grandma's heart, but she wasn't at her best those last few years. In addition to grieving the most stable person in her life, I think Anna's struggled to come to terms with the fact that her grandma wasn't perfect."

My heart kicked into an unsteady beat, and my chest felt tight. I didn't like thinking about how worried Anna must be and what this year must've been like for her.

Eloise's question punctured my thoughts. "What are you going to do, Jasper?"

"Now, isn't that the question of the day?" I replied with a shrug. "I'm not sure. Originally, I intended to come here and persuade Anna to sign off on letting me sell my half. Now, I'm not so sure."

Next thing I knew, Eloise was flinging her arms around me and giving me a fierce hug. She stepped back before I could even fully wrap my brain around what was happening. "I knew you weren't just a grumpy old boy."

"Old boy? Doesn't that cancel itself out?" I quipped.

Eloise rolled her eyes. "No, it suits you perfectly. You're young, but you act like an old man inside—all cynical and kind of bitter. I'd love to know a little bit more about your childhood."

At that moment, the winery phone rang loudly, saving me from that potentially awkward conversation.

Eloise swung away. "Duty calls. Be nice to Anna." With that sharp reminder, she hurried over to take the phone call.

I decided to leave Anna alone for the time being and headed out for a drive. Not much later, I found myself parked on the side of the highway, looking out over the Pacific Ocean as the sun set in a glorious explosion of color—tangerine, gold, and pink brushing together. Nature really outdid herself here.

My cell phone rang, and I looked at the screen on my dashboard to see my cousin's name flashing. "Hi, Simon," I said, answering quickly.

"Jasper! Rumor has it you're in the States," Simon replied.

"For once, rumor is correct. I was intending to get in touch with you and stop by on my way back."

Simon was a cousin from my mother's side of the family. He was happily married and living outside of New York City with his American wife.

"Where are you exactly?" he asked. "Bridget and I would love to see you."

"I'm in California. I'm sure it won't surprise you to learn my grandfather had a trick up his sleeve in his will. Apparently, he owned half of a winery and flower business out here in California. I have no need of that business interest, but I couldn't even consider selling it without spending a month on the property and getting a written agreement from the other owner to let me sell. So here I am."

Simon chuckled. "Well then, sounds interesting. Nothing wrong with a winery. You could use a little extra wine to loosen you up."

He couldn't see me, but I rolled my eyes. "Of course. How are you and Bridget?"

"We're great. Actually, I have a week off coming up. We could visit you. It might be fun."

I briefly wondered what Anna would think and decided I didn't care. I thought she might actually like Bridget and Simon and maybe not be so prickly with me.

"Sounds like a grand plan. Would Brendan come with you?" I asked, referring to his stepson.

"On short notice, probably not. We can see if he can stay with Bridget's parents."

"Got it. Well, I can't commit to saying we have room here, but I'm sure I can find you a local place to stay. Why don't I send you the information? I'll email it."

"Go for it. Who's the co-owner?"

"Anna, Anna Lennon. My suspicion is my grandfather was in love with her grandmother, and that's how this all came about."

"Like some kind of late in life affair?" Simon teased.

"Seeing as both of them were widowed, I don't think that was the case. I think rather they fell in love when she attended a semester of college in London. There's correspondence dating back to then. It's all suspicion on my part," I replied.

"It's a story, and those are always more fun. Nothing is ever a coincidence. You know that, right?"

Nothing is ever a coincidence. You know that, right?

. . .

Simon's philosophical question echoed in my thoughts when I returned to the loft flat above the winery. Anna was standing in the kitchen, stirring something on the stove and sipping a glass of red wine. The moment my eyes clapped on her, need jolted me so hard, my knees went weak for a moment.

ANNA

Jasper walked in the room, and the sound of the door clicking shut behind him pinged a little echo in my body. He had this strange effect on me, where every sensation felt highlighted, almost as if each one was echoing and multiplying.

I'd pulled myself together after getting upset earlier and was no longer an emotionally reactive mess. I'd decided to cook because that was one thing guaranteed to soothe me. I turned down the flame under the sauce I was stirring and glanced over at him.

His eyes met mine from across the room, and it felt as if sparks scattered through the air between us, instantly sending a wash of heat rolling through me from head to toe. I grabbed my glass of wine and took a gulp, almost in desperation.

Perhaps that was why I'd been such an emotional wreck ever since he'd arrived unexpectedly. I wasn't used to having this kind of forceful physical reaction to a man. I liked to think I generally had my shit together, but Jasper's presence had this way of making me feel as if I was spiraling out of control. Because, despite my best efforts, I couldn't reel in my raw desire for him.

"Hello," he said, dipping his head slightly as he crossed the room to stand beside the counter.

"Hey," I said, smiling too brightly. "I'm making dinner. Are you hungry?"

His eyes skimmed my face and then flicked over to the stove. When his gaze bounced back to mine, I felt a little jolt. "I'm always hungry," he replied.

"Always?"

He shrugged lightly. "I am a man."

"Oh, is constant hunger limited to men?"

His lips quirked in a smile, and my belly flipped, butterflies spinning inside. "I suppose not. Wouldn't want to lean on gender stereotypes now, would we? What are you making?" he asked.

"Pasta with fresh tomato sauce. I promise it'll be delicious. I even have some fresh mozzarella cheese."

"Anna, you don't need to make promises about your food. Everything you make is delicious. You're spoiling me."

For some reason, that gave me a flash of pride. "Really? With your money, I imagine you've eaten at all the best restaurants in London. This is just a small winery in California where we serve hors d'oeuvres with wine tastings."

He looked at me quietly. "Perhaps I have eaten in plenty of nice restaurants, but rest assured, the food here is stiff competition. Can I help?"

Flustered, I looked down, my eyes scanning what I'd already done. "I don't think so. I'm just waiting for the water to boil. Would you like something to drink?"

"What are my choices?"

I didn't know why, but this rather mundane and innocent conversation felt heated. Turning, I gestured vaguely toward the wine rack. "There's wine. I have some beer too if you'd like."

"That might be nice. It's been a hot day."

He opened the refrigerator and got a beer after I pointed him that way. My eyes lingered on his throat as he tilted his head back and swallowed. My mouth watered because I knew what he tasted like, and I wanted to drag my tongue along his neck. Jasper was a very lickable man.

He lowered the bottle of beer, his gaze considering as he regarded me. "I found something."

I heard the water start to boil and turned to pour the pasta in and give it a stir as I asked, "What's that?"

"Your grandmother forgot about a retirement account set up by your grandfather. You can buy me out if you want to."

I stared at Jasper, slowly lowering the slotted spoon. "What?" My brain wasn't computing.

"Your grandmother lost track of a retirement account set up by your grandfather. You were listed as the next beneficiary if your grandmother passed away. With that, you can afford to buy me out," he repeated.

I should've felt overjoyed, but I was a combination of stunned and flummoxed. This was so unexpected that I didn't even know what my reaction should be.

As I stared at him blankly, a slow smile stretched across Jasper's face, softening his sharp features. "I can surmise I've surprised you." He took another swallow of his beer as those butterflies spun madly in my belly.

"You could say that," I finally managed. "I don't even know what to think."

He set his beer bottle on the counter, tracing a circle around it with his fingertip. "I would've thought you'd be jumping up and down."

All my insecurities scrambled to the forefront of my mind because I knew it wasn't as simple as buying Jasper out. I needed to get the business back on solid footing. My heart was pounding, and nervousness was making my chest tight, but I decided to be honest.

"I'm excited, but I don't know if that's the best plan. If I use that money to buy you out, then I don't know where I'll get the money to clean up all the other bills I owe on."

His brows hitched up before he nodded slowly. "Excellent point."

"What exactly is your job?"

"Apparently, here I help feed the goats and chickens, I serve wine, and I go through old files," he replied. His lips kicked up in a slow grin.

Jasper smiling in any way was *not* good for my sanity. When his otherwise somber features softened and his eyes twinkled, a fizzy sense of joy rose through my body, mingling with the heat and ever-present desire that I couldn't seem to squelch no matter how hard I tried.

Feeling my cheeks heat, I looked down and needlessly stirred pasta as the water rolled at a boil. "I mean, your job in London," I clarified.

"Ah. I work in my grandfather's company, which is now mine, but it's hard to remember that. Believe it or not, I'm an accountant. I specialize in forensic accounting."

"What's that? I hear forensic, and I think of those crime shows."

His chuckle sent a hot shiver chasing over my skin. "That's far more glamorous and exciting than what I do. I chase numbers and dig into things to find out what people want to keep hidden. I always loved numbers when I was a kid. My grandfather encouraged it because he knew it would serve his purposes. I don't mind that it served his purposes."

"So you're an accountant? But you own the company now?"

He shrugged. "Yes. Technically, I was his chief financial officer. Now that he passed away, I'm the CEO, so numbers aren't all I do."

"Well, of course you found that retirement account then," I commented.

"That wasn't a given. I suppose I might've eventually found it, but I found it because the statements were in the files we got from your grandparents' old house."

I turned off the burner under the pasta and busied myself getting the food ready. I didn't know what else to say about the money he'd discovered suddenly at my disposal. Whenever I was nervous or uncertain, I focused on things I could do well. Cooking was definitely one of them.

Not much later, Jasper was sitting across from me at the counter. "This is beautiful," he said when he looked over at me.

It was, if I did say so myself. On cream-colored pottery plates, the bright red marinara sauce was a pretty contrast to the garnish of fresh basil. I took a bite, savoring the creamy mozzarella.

We ate quietly, and Jasper leaned back after he'd cleaned his plate completely. "I think you're going to fatten me up, Anna."

I laughed. "Somehow, I doubt it."

I stood and took his plate to put in the dishwasher with mine. He came around the counter, commenting, "I'll help clean up."

Before I could shoo him away, he was already lifting the pans I'd left on the stove top and rinsing them in the sink to hand to me. The activity was so mundane and oddly intimate. I still didn't know how to read him or interpret anything in the situation. I'd been resisting the urge while we ate to ask him what he wanted to do about the business. I knew, obviously, he had come here with the intention to ask me to agree to him selling his half. But I didn't know if that had changed.

Moments later, I found myself standing by the windows looking out over the field. The sun had already set. It was that almost magical time of dusk when it wasn't light but not yet fully dark. Jasper had taken a phone call and stepped into his bedroom. Normally, about now, I would curl up on the couch and watch whatever TV show happened to be on. Or I would be anxiously trying to solve the riddle of how to climb out of the debt my grandmother had left behind.

As soon as I heard the door open, I spun around, my arms wrapped tightly around my waist. "Do you still want to sell your half?" My question came tumbling out rapidly. I needed to know.

Jasper looked startled when his eyes met mine from across the room. He didn't answer right away. As he walked toward me, it felt as if there were a cord between us, cinching tighter and tighter with each step, the tension fraught with desire, with my anxieties, with my confusion about the depth of attraction to this man, and all of it banging into each other.

He stopped a few feet away, his eyes holding mine. "Well?" I prompted, my voice coming out a little husky.

"I don't know," he finally said, each word measured. He sounded almost confused.

Relief gusted through me, and I felt almost silly and giddy. "What do you mean you don't know?" I pressed.

"It doesn't feel right to leave you in the lurch. And you have an excellent point. You have much better uses for that money. I don't know why I'm saying 'I don't know.'" His eyes shifted from mine, looking past my shoulder through the windows. "What are those sparks of light?"

Turning, I saw the inky sky glittering with fireflies. I felt Jasper's presence like the wind buffeting me fiercely when he came to stand beside me. He emanated strength and heat, and I felt slick need throb at the apex of my thighs. I was a needy girl when it came to him.

"Those are fireflies," I murmured, my voice falling into the quiet, charged air around us. "Why don't you know?" I couldn't let this go, apparently. Turning, I looked at him.

After what felt like forever, his eyes caught mine before sweeping down and back up my body. Everywhere his eyes landed felt like drops of lava on my skin.

"I don't know why I don't know," he said slowly. "Apparently, I can't treat this like a business decision."

"Is that what it is, a business decision?"

"It should be. It's become complicated."

"How?"

"You."

"Me?"

"Yes, Anna. *You.* I have no business wanting you, but I do."

All of a sudden, I thought bad decisions were a great idea. "Well, I guess we're in agreement on that."

"On what?"

"I have no business wanting you, but I do," I parroted his words back at him.

Jasper's eyes went dark, and my pulse began to race as my belly trembled. I practically had to squeeze my thighs together to ease the ache there.

Chapter Twenty-One

JASPER

The list of reasons for why I should've been sensible here was definitive. But I didn't stand a chance. Not with my cock so swollen I could feel the heavy weight of it when Anna's cheeks went pink, and I wanted to count all the freckles scattered there. Not when I saw the barely perceptible shift of her thighs and remembered how slick, hot, and wet she'd been the other night. Not when I wanted to be sheathed inside her sweetness.

The moment caught, and sparks charged the air between us. I held myself in check. I needed for her to be the one to make this move.

She stared at me, and I waited. Just when I thought she wasn't going to, she closed the distance between us, stopping right in front of me. She smelled like flowers. When she lifted her hand and her fingertips trailed along my jaw, I held my breath. She curled her hand around the back of my neck to bring my mouth to hers, and I couldn't hold back a low growl as my entire body absorbed the shock to my system.

The moment Anna's tongue slicked against mine, I was gone. Kissing her was intoxicating. She yanked my control away, and everything got *real* hot, *real* fast.

Just like the last time I kissed her, everything happened fast. It was as if someone left the latch open on a gate and let loose a herd of horses. Fierce need galloped through me, and my hand tangled in her hair as I tugged her against me in a full-body clench.

Her mouth was hungry and sweet, her lips mobile as her tongue glided sensually against mine. She made a soft sound at the back of her throat, the sound sizzling through me and setting my nerve endings on fire.

I lost track of the moment. All I knew was the feel of her soft breasts pressing against me and the way her bottom gave under my touch when I slid my palm down to cup it and pull her tight against my aching arousal. For a man who had no business kissing this girl, there was absolutely nothing businesslike about what we were doing. Her hands splayed on my chest, mapping the muscles before she reached between us and boldly stroked my cock through my jeans.

I drew back from her sweet mouth to gulp in air. "Sweetheart," I began, my breath hissing through my teeth when she stroked me again.

"I'm not feeling very sweet," she murmured, the naughty lilt in her voice like a bolt of lightning in my body.

I tugged at her blouse, gratified when the buttons gave way easily. Yet again, I discovered Anna had a penchant for sexy underwear. Today, I was greeted by the sight of a cream lace bra with her nipples barely concealed behind it, pink and pebbled.

I was leaning down to cup one, my teeth grazing over the taut bead, but Anna had other priorities. She popped open the buttons on my fly, sliding her hand down into my boxers, and let out a satisfied hum when her palm made contact with my hard, hot length.

I gave her nipple a suck before I lifted my head, and murmured, "Slow—"

"I'm not slowing down," she countered with a saucy grin before she shoved my jeans and boxers down, and my cock sprang free.

She was sexy all on her own, but throw in her bossiness with that saucy grin, and I was treading in territory of losing all control. Her smooth palm curled around my length, giving me a light stroke before her thumb smeared across the tip, wiping the drop of pre-cum rolling out.

I usually set the tone when it came to sexual encounters, but Anna was having none of it. I started to say her name again, but all that came out was a rough groan when she leaned down and took my crown in her mouth. Her tongue swirled around the tip, and then she sucked me in deep as I grasped her hair.

Fuck me. Anna's mouth was pure magic. She teased me with her tongue and then sucked me in again and again, taking me deep before drawing back. My release was threatening as electricity sizzled down my spine. This wasn't how I wanted to lose control, not just yet.

I managed to get her entire name out through gritted teeth. She rocked back on her heels and looked up at me. Her strawberry curls were in a messy rumple around her shoulders.

"Now, it's your turn to do as I say," I murmured as I reached down and grabbed one of her hands. Her lips curled in another saucy smile as she straightened.

"Okay." Two syllables said in her throaty voice, and I felt the hot shot straight to my balls.

I turned, and she followed right behind me. I stopped just in front of the bathroom door, which was immediately between her bedroom door and mine. "Whose bed?"

Anna gave me a long look, catching her bottom lip in her teeth and distracting me immediately. I *had* to kiss her again. Next thing I knew, we were tumbling into another blur of kisses when I took sip after greedy sip of her lips, soft, plump, and pliant, as her sassy tongue tangled with mine.

It was only when I broke free for a nearly desperate gasp of air that she answered, "Mine."

In another second, we were in her bedroom. Our clothes dropped on the floor, falling in a messy rumple on the floor scattered around us. Then I was nudging her back with my hands on her hips. I forced myself to go still for a moment when her hips bumped against the bed.

I had only been fantasizing about Anna naked for an entire week and a half. In the larger scheme of time, that was nothing more than a blink. But for me, those fantasies had filled my thoughts so thoroughly the time felt endless.

She had freckles scattered on her shoulders, a few on her belly, and more scattered like far-flung stars on her legs, all cinnamon brown and tiny. I thought perhaps if I kissed every single one, then I would be able to map her body and make her mine.

She had plump breasts, a trim waist with a soft curve to her belly, and generous hips. Speaking of hips, I slid my hands down the dip in her waist to grip her hips and push her back on the bed.

"How come your bed?" I asked.

I gripped her calves, pushing her knees apart as I made my way up. "Better pillows," she gasped right as I teased my fingers into her pink, glistening pussy.

"Are you telling me you gave me inferior pillows? I think you owe me."

I sank two fingers deep inside her, everything in my body lunging, straining with her when her head fell back, and her hips rocked into my touch. I blew lightly on her sex, reveling in how she trembled under my touch as I stroked into her again.

"Wha-at do I owe you?" she gasped.

"Mmm, I think perhaps an orgasm, maybe two." Then I brought my mouth to her, licking through the salty tang of her arousal, and she shuddered all over.

Fuck me. Anna was so responsive, and not the least bit shy. Once we had our hands on each other, nothing held us back. I was far more accustomed to women worrying about how they looked and being careful and controlled in their responses. In contrast, she was loud and abandoned, almost messy.

I didn't get to tease her for long. I saw her hands curling into fists, and she gasped my name before her pussy rippled around my fingers when I sucked her clit lightly. She actually cried out my name, and an unfamiliar possessiveness reverberated inside me when she did. I was too caught up in the moment to dwell on it although it was as if a small bell rang inside.

I was rising, pressing my knee into the mattress when I realized I needed a condom. I was off the bed and striding into my room in a second. "Where are you going?" Anna called, sounding impatient.

"Condom," I called over my shoulder. I made it to my room where I snatched one out of my toiletry bag.

I might've broken land speed records on

the way back. I was sheathed and then finally sinking into the cradle of her hips.

"Hurry," she ordered, curling her legs around my hips.

And I hurried, belying any illusions I had about being in control of this. The moment I sank into her satiny, snug core, my mind simply went blank.

Chapter Twenty-Two

ANNA

I stared up at Jasper. His face was cast half in shadow, and his eyes were intent on mine. This was supposed to be sex. It was definitely that, but it was wildly out of control, hot, fast, and messy. Jasper was British and proper, and this was not what I expected of him.

But then, this wasn't what I expected of myself. He turned me into a little seductress. I had no shame with raw, carnal need driving me.

His weight settled over me, and the muscles of the shoulders bunched. "Hold on," he murmured.

Like a good girl, I did just that, curling my legs more tightly around his hips. He rocked back and filled me again, the stretch delicious and intoxicating. I let out a ragged sigh of pure pleasure.

Before I realized what was happening, he efficiently rolled us over so I was sitting astride him, and he was propped up on the pillows. He leaned forward, catching one of my nipples with his lips and giving it a sharp suck, the pleasure arrowing straight to my core.

"Now, I know you like to be in charge, so..."

I needed no further instruction. Holding onto his shoulders, I rose up and sank down slowly, savoring every inch of him as he filled me. My control lasted for all of one second before I was rocking restlessly, and he was arching into me as we took turns pushing higher and higher.

I barely heard him speak through the thrum of my pulse buzzing. "You owe me two orgasms."

With a hot, open kiss on my neck, he reached between us, working magic with his fingers just over my clit. He caught my lips with his when I came, the shudders hitting my body so hard, I barely registered anything but the decadence of pleasure slamming through me.

I was still reverberating when I felt his

hand tightening in my hair as he let out a rough cry with my name following. I collapsed on him, just like the other night on the couch. Just like that time, he held me close.

I didn't remember if we talked after that, but I did remember him holding me by the hand and leading me into the shower. My legs were unsteady, and I felt like I'd melted. I did remember hot water raining over us and noticing that he had a tattoo curling around his hip in bold black strokes. I also remembered him laughing as the soap bubbles rolled over my skin, and he teased me to another climax with his fingers.

We fell asleep together, and I came awake with the feel of his hot lips on the back of my neck. I rolled over to have his mouth claim mine in a sweet, hungry kiss.

Yeah, so I could totally get used to that kind of waking up. I could also totally get used to sleeping tangled up with Jasper. Turned out, he was a cuddler. Who knew?

The British big shot was flipping my expectations upside down. After yet another two orgasms, I made us omelets for breakfast. I wasn't sure how to interact with him after that wild night, but somehow, we eased into a regular morning.

Although nothing about the situation was regular. We were into the second week of his month here, and I still wondered what he would want to do at the end of it. I knew, technically, I had a little power in the situation. He couldn't sell without my written permission, even if I were the one buying him out. It's just I didn't want to be business partners with someone who didn't want to be in the situation. Especially now that he knew I could buy him out.

Fortunately, it was a flower day. I needed something to keep me busy after last night. Jasper was in the middle of a phone conference as I was getting ready to leave. He held a finger up from where he sat at my desk. I was just reaching for my straw hat and lowered my arm. "Yes?"

"Do you need any help?"

I was still confused by how helpful he was trying to be. He honestly seemed to think he might as well work since he was here. I shook my head. "No. We have a system. I'm sure you have plenty of work to catch up on. You can count on it being quiet up here."

He held my gaze for several long beats before nodding. "I'll be down at some point." Another pause, and my belly shimmied. "Thank you for breakfast."

"Of course."

I had to willfully tear my eyes from his. I practically ran out of the loft apartment. As soon as I made it downstairs, I was pulled into the day. Customers were already arriving to wander through the flower fields. The weather was perfect, sunny with a light breeze. By the time late afternoon rolled around, I was exhausted but happy.

"Here you go," I said, handing over a bouquet.

The young man smiled. "She's going to love these. How much are they?"

"Twenty dollars." I tapped open my computer tablet. "We take cash or credit cards."

The man handed over a credit card, and I quickly swiped it. "What's the occasion?" I asked conversationally.

He suddenly looked nervous, a twitch of worry appearing between his brows. "I'm asking her to marry me. I've got flowers, a bottle of wine I got from your winery, and the ring."

At that moment, the back of my neck prickled, and I knew Jasper was approaching. My body's awareness and responsiveness to him was shocking. I kept my attention on the young man. "Oh, that's lovely! It sounds like you've planned everything. Are you taking her out to dinner?"

Jasper arrived beside me at the table. We handled transactions for the greenhouse and flowers with a table we set up each week right outside the gates that led into the flower fields. It was temporary but more convenient than having traffic going in and out of the winery.

"I've got a picnic," the young man said.

"A picnic for what?" Jasper interjected.

Just the sound of his voice sent a little shiver through me.

"He's proposing," I said, glancing up toward Jasper. "He has flowers, wine, and a ring. I think he's set himself up for success."

Jasper looked at the man solemnly for a moment before smiling. "It sounds like it. Best of luck."

"Please do come back and let us know how it goes," I said as I handed over the computer tablet, gesturing for where he could sign with his fingertip.

After he signed, he looked up. "I definitely will."

After he walked off, I felt suddenly tongue-tied. That was another thing Jasper did to me. I never knew what to say, and now, we'd taken things to a whole new level last night. I didn't know what that meant. I thought I needed to treat it casually because anything else seemed insane.

"It's been busy," Jasper commented as he looked around. There were still a few customers left but not many. Eloise was chatting with a couple in the perennial section, and our rooster let out his distinctive call.

"Flower day is always busy."

I busied myself tidying up the table. "If you don't mind me asking, how is it that your grandparents ended up with this combination winery and flower business?" Jasper asked. Without me asking, he began picking up debris scattered around the table.

As I put receipts in a box, I replied, "Well, my grandparents had the flowers first because both of them loved gardening. Just for fun and personal reasons, they started growing grapes and making wine. My grandmother was the one who eventually turned the wine into part of the business. She was an early adopter before local wines got really popular. I honestly think that led to some of her financial mistakes. The money was just so easy at the beginning."

I closed the cashbox and looked over at Jasper. His eyes were considering as he looked back at me before nodding slowly.

"Makes sense. You don't have to worry as much. You know it's going to be fine, right?"

Staring at him, I knew intellectually his words made sense, but "fine" was something I felt as if I'd been chasing my entire life. I didn't want much. Just stability and to be able to sleep without anxiety running laps and chasing my thoughts in circles at night. "Maybe," I said, looking down quickly.

Looking up at the sound of tires on the gravel, I watched as the last vehicle departed the parking lot. Eloise came over to the table. "I'm gonna head home. Everything's already locked down in the winery. Do you need any help feeding the chickens and the goats before I go?"

"Oh, no. I've got it. Thank you for everything today."

Eloise smiled at us. "All right. See you tomorrow."

She disappeared around the winery into the parking area for staff. I stood from the table. "I'll carry the stuff in and then go take care of the animals."

"I'll help," Jasper said.

"You don't have to—"

One of Jasper's brows rose in a dark slash. "I'm not going to stand around while you do all the work, Anna."

Without another word, he handed me the cash box and gathered up the other items on the table. "Where does everything go?"

"Oh, in the storage area in the back of the kitchen. Follow me."

He was quiet as we crossed the parking area. After we put away what we had in our hands, he helped with the table and folding chairs while I organized the receipts for Eloise so she could tally everything up tomorrow when she came in.

I thought I would be able to feed the animals in peace. It was work, technically, but it relaxed me, especially after a busy day like today. My nerves were on high alert with Jasper around. The entire situation was making me feel slightly insane.

The past year had stretched my coping mechanisms to their limit between dealing with my grief from Gram's death and facing the unsettling financial situation she'd left behind. I didn't like talking about it. I'd already been scrambling to find a way out of the mess before he showed up.

Jasper with his clear preference to persuade me to let him sell. Jasper with his ridiculously handsome self. I wanted to blame him for my attraction to him, but that didn't seem exactly fair.

Then I'd set my nerves on scramble when I kissed him. Now, I didn't know if my nerves would ever return to normal as long as he was around. I'd like to think that maybe we'd dampened the flaming conflagration between us after last night. But in my case, not even a little. I flushed all over just thinking about him. Add in his magic fingers, lips, and tongue and my body hummed. I thought his cock was even magic.

With that thought, I snorted to myself as I crossed over to check on the chickens behind the barn. Sex had never really blown me away, but sex with Jasper blew me away.

"Hey, girls," I called as I stepped in through the gate.

I heard footsteps and turned to see Jasper walking toward me. "I said I was going to help," he called.

"Oh, okay. Do you want to check on the goats?"

He caught my eyes, his lips teasing with a grin. "Sure, I'd love to check on the goats, Anna. Can you promise me Jasper's not going to shove me into a puddle?"

Heat flashed through me with my laughter and the naughty glint in his eyes. "I can't make any promises as far as the goats.

You know where their feed is. I'll be right in to help."

After scattering the chicken feed for the girls, I made sure their water was fresh, then even took the extra time to change out the hay in their nesting spots. Of course, it was good for the chickens, but it also bought me some time. I didn't quite know what to do with myself around him.

After they were all settled in, I made my way into the barn to find Jasper nowhere in sight. The goats were long gone too.

Uh-oh. Jasper and Tinker Bell could be mischievous.

I hurried out to the parking lot to find Jasper running, actually running, through one of the flower fields. I couldn't see Tinker Bell and Jasper the goat, but I could guess where they were based on the motion of the flowers.

Chapter Twenty-Three

JASPER

"You..." I paused, trying to choose the best word. "Goat," I finally said with a hand on my hip.

I wasn't out of breath, but my heart rate was humming along after that little jog chasing these two imps out of the barn.

Tinker Bell eyed me and then lowered her head and bumped her forehead into my ankle. Today, she was wearing a pink sweater. Never one to be left out of the fun, my namesake—whether he was or not was beside the point—burst out of the tall grass and rammed me in the back of the knee just enough to make my knees buckle, and I stumbled.

"Jasper! Tinker Bell!" Anna was on the way to handle this.

I had no idea why, but I didn't like the idea of her thinking I couldn't deal with two small goats. They were just goats, one of which was wearing a pink sweater, and the other a navy sweater with white polka dots.

"All right, goats," I began, using my sternest voice. "We're going back to the barn. Who likes food?"

Tinker Bell bit the toe of my shoe in response.

Anna arrived beside me, breathlessly cute. "I'm so sorry," she said quickly, brushing her hair out of her face.

I didn't know where her straw hat went, but Anna sent a sizzle of lust through me with her curls rumpled, her cheeks flushed, and her lips parted as she caught her breath. Bloody hell. We were in the middle of a field, and there were two goats running amok, and all I could think about was how much I wanted her.

She held up two leads. "They won't follow you back."

"I got it," I said when she moved to walk past me. I took the two leads from her, ignoring her curious gaze. When I leaned over to clip Tinker Bell on her lead, she dodged me at the last minute, running right back into the grass.

"All right then," I said to Jasper. "We share a name. You're reasonable. Now let's get you back to get some food." I didn't let myself think about how ridiculous it was that I was carrying on a conversation with a goat in a polka-dotted sweater.

Jasper stood docilely beside me as I leaned over to clip on the lead. I experienced a flash of victory, but then he took off, so fast the lead slapped against my legs with a hard snap.

I bit back a sigh. Anna snorted, and when I looked over, she was biting her bottom lip to keep from laughing too hard. I straightened and shrugged. "Go ahead and laugh."

She threw her head back with a throaty laugh, and that lust, inconvenient and entirely out of place, surged through me again. She ended with a giggle.

"Please do tell me how you capture miniature goats."

Anna let out a whistle and reached into the pocket of her skirt to pull out two treats. In another moment, the tall grass rustled nearby, and the two naughty goats appeared, trotting right over and taking the treats. She handed me the lead belonging to Jasper, clipped the other lead on Tinker Bell, and we walked back together.

After we fed the goats and began walking across the parking lot to the winery, I caught myself almost reaching to hold Anna's hand. I'd gone from having no business to doing what I was doing with her to flat-out losing my mind. I'd been legitimately busy all day today, catching up on emails and documents related to business, yet I'd stolen glance after glance out the windows. Every time my eyes landed on Anna, I would get impatient for when we could be alone again.

I didn't hold her hand. We headed upstairs, and she went to shower while I debated whether to barge in and join her. I didn't do that, either. I had some sense, after all.

My phone rang while she was in the shower. When I saw Simon's name on the screen, I answered, "Hello."

"Hi, Jasper. I'm calling with an update. We have tickets. We'll landing this weekend, and we're getting a car rental. I found a bed and breakfast only a mile away from where you're staying."

"Well, that sounds great. I didn't realize you'd be here that soon. I need to let Anna know you're coming."

"You don't need to entertain us." Simon paused and chuckled. "Actually, I expect you to entertain us but not your business partner. We'd love a tour of the winery because I'm sure it would be lovely, but we can find plenty of things to do."

"I'll make sure I'm available. It's been a while, so it'll be good to see you both."

"Perfect. Bridget's looking forward to it. It'll be good. I think it's been, what? A year since I saw you," Simon replied just as Anna came out of the bathroom.

"Thereabouts. I was in New York last year for business, and we had dinner."

"I hope you're actually taking some time to relax."

We said our goodbyes, and I turned the ringer off on my phone, setting it on the desk beside my laptop. Anna had gone into her bedroom to change, and I was fighting against the pull to go in there. It seemed no matter where she was, there was a magnetic force that was hard for me to ignore.

A moment later, she reappeared. Her hair was damp, and her skin was flushed from her shower. I wanted to kiss her. She had this fresh, sun-kissed look to her.

"There's some leftover pizza downstairs

that I made at lunch," she commented. "Would you like some for dinner?"

"Haven't you figured out yet that I don't turn down any food from you?"

That was how I found myself enjoying her delicious pizza—with fresh goat mozzarella cheese, tomatoes from the garden, and basil and spinach—in the front area of the winery where they held the wine tastings. The setting sun outside served as a lovely backdrop. Anna had turned on the lights above the bar. After we finished eating, she sat on the bar in a lightweight cotton skirt with a T-shirt. Her feet were bare, and her toenails painted purple.

My hips were resting against the counter beside her. I'd not spent one penny for this night, and it was one of the best nights I'd ever had. A main point of conversation: the goats.

"You have to find their favorite things, and that's how you bribe them," she said with a solemn nod as if imparting very important information.

Which I supposed it was. "Food then?" I asked

"Of course. They're so cute, and they never fail to make me smile."

"I have to agree there. It's the goat-guaranteed smile."

Anna giggled, and the sound spun round me, my heart tightening slightly before shifting into a rolling beat.

Her eyes caught mine, and in a flash, our humor had died. The air around us felt electric, the moment stretching tight. I wanted to kiss her. I wanted to do that a lot.

As I finally gave in to the urge, it was pure relief the moment my lips met hers. Her hand lightly cupped my jaw with her fingertips trailing down my neck. Her mouth was warm and sweet, and I could taste the red wine we'd just shared.

With Anna, every touch was an experience in and of itself. I wasn't so focused on a specific goal. I was utterly present in every moment along the way.

She let out a sigh when I broke free of her sweet mouth and dropped hot kisses on the side of her neck. When I cupped her breast through her cotton shirt and discovered she wasn't wearing a bra, I murmured, "Fuck me, Anna."

She giggled. "I think we're on the way to that."

Chapter Twenty-Four

ANNA

The wood of the counter was cool under my back while the rest of me was on fire. Jasper and his magic mouth had just brought me to orgasm. Right here. In the winery.

Now, he was driving into me with deep, purposeful strokes, and my next orgasm was already spiraling. Pleasure tightened to an almost unbearable pressure.

Although this encounter was slightly less rushed and insane than last night, we were both half-dressed. I could feel the abrasion of his jeans on the insides of my thighs. My skirt was bunched around my hips. I had managed to get his shirt off, which was freaking awesome because Jasper's chest was all hard muscle pressed against me. His elbows were propped beside my shoulders.

"Anna," he murmured, his gruff British whisper sending my belly into a series of flips, even in the middle of crazy hot sex.

Opening my eyes, I was immediately trapped in the beam of his intent gaze. He rocked inside me again, creating a teasing pressure over my clit. When I whimpered, he reached down and teased his fingers over my slippery sex.

Everything drew tight in my center and then snapped, sending shockwaves of pleasure through me. I heard Jasper growl my name and felt him shaking against me.

After that, there was nothing but the sound of our ragged breathing and me trying to find some dignity in the situation. I thought perhaps there was none. I'd just let a man I'd only known for less than two weeks take me in my own winery. I'd been so lost in the experience that we could've had an audience and I wouldn't have cared.

Jasper kept surprising me, and he did so again. He eased me up and helped me set my clothes to rights. The cool tile of the floor under my bare feet anchored me as I looked up into his eyes.

He was quiet, his eyes considering, before he began, "I didn't plan for this."

"Do you plan for everything?" I interjected.

Chapter Twenty-Five

JASPER

There were many things I didn't plan. Although if given the choice, I *did* like to plan for everything.

On that list of things I didn't plan for: getting head butted by Jasper. "Dude," I commented as I looked down at him.

The little goat looked up at me, blinking his eyes before dashing away and kicking his back feet up in the air while wearing goat pajamas. Today, he sported a lavender onesie with dark purple hearts.

Tinker Bell eyed me dispassionately and continued munching on her pile of hay. "Wow, this is not what I expected."

Turning, I found my cousin Simon strolling into the barn. He stopped beside me, his brows hitching up. "Good to see you, cuz." He burst out laughing and gave me a quick back-slapping hug. Stepping back, after he stopped laughing, he commented, "You forgot to mention the goats."

I chuckled as I looked down at Jasper who had just returned to head butt me in the calves again. "Oh, did I forget to mention them? This is Jasper, and that's Tinker Bell," I explained, gesturing between them.

Simon started laughing again. When he finished, he asked, "Jasper? Is he named after you?"

"To my knowledge, no. He was named before Anna even met me. Where is Bridget?"

"In the winery talking to Anna, your business partner. Anna told me you were out here feeding the goats, and I couldn't resist coming to see the spectacle."

"Yes, I was feeding the goats. It's not so bad. I'll follow you back in."

Simon fell into step beside me as we left the barn. I made sure the gate was firmly locked so Tinker Bell and Jasper didn't escape from the small paddock just outside the barn.

"How was the trip?" I asked.

"Uneventful. We got on a plane in New York and landed in San Francisco. Beautiful drive here from San Francisco, though."

"It is. You'll have to make sure to take a trip along the coastal highway. It's stunning."

"We're already planning on it. So how are things? What's your plan?" Simon prompted.

I stopped just beyond the flower trellis that led to the path into the winery entrance. "I have no idea," I said honestly.

Simon looked surprised, his alert gaze holding mine. "Not going to be the cutthroat businessman as usual? This," he said, gesturing toward the winery, the flower fields, and the barn where the chickens and goats lived, "isn't exactly your typical type of business."

"I know." I ran a hand through my hair. "The way grandfather set it up, I need Anna's written permission to sell my half, and I need to spend a month here."

"Here?" Simon pressed, his brows hitching up.

"Yes. I have to stay here on the premises."

"Well, that's interesting. Is Anna willing to let you sell?"

"I think she'd rather I didn't. Actually, to be clear, I think she'd rather we weren't in this situation. It's complicated."

Bridget appeared in the doorway to the winery, swinging it open. "Jasper!" she called.

Turning, I approached with Simon following beside me. "Hello, dear," I said, pulling her into a quick hug. "How was your trip?"

"It was great. This place is awesome. Simon, you have to taste this wine." She looped her hand through his elbow as she tugged him over to the counter where Anna was standing with several bottles of wine and glasses on the counter.

Closing the door behind us, I followed them over. "The wine here is amazing," I offered.

"It's incredible," Bridget said, casting a warm smile to Anna.

Anna's cheeks flushed slightly, and she smiled. "Thank you. We try."

"Which one should I taste?" Simon asked, glancing from Anna to me.

"They're all good. Consider this your personal wine tasting event," I teased.

As Simon tasted several of the wines, I had a hard time not thinking about what Anna and I had done last night on this very counter, with her skirt bunched around her hips and me sinking inside her clenching heat.

No, I didn't plan any of this, especially not Anna. I felt as if my grandfather was playing a massive joke from the grave, and the joke was definitely on me. Because I couldn't think straight when it came to Anna.

"Wow, this one is delicious. Do you all ship?" Simon asked.

He looked at me, as if somehow I would know the answer to that question. In turn, I looked toward Anna. "I don't know. Do we ship?"

She cleared her throat. "Occasionally. That part of our business hasn't really gotten off the ground for retail. We sell wholesale to distributors, but we don't have a website for retail sales. That's on my endless list of things to do."

"I can set that up." Three pairs of eyes swung in my direction. "I can," I said with a light shrug. I didn't want to contemplate what it meant that I was offering to do that.

"You have a stakc in this business so you should. I'm telling you right now if you all sell online and formulate a strong marketing plan, this will rack up a profit for you," Simon said firmly.

"Which one is your favorite?" Bridget asked Simon.

"I actually like this one best," he replied, tapping his finger on a bottle without a label.

Anna smiled, her cheeks going pink and sending a hot bolt of need sizzling through me. Bloody hell. All the girl had to do was blush and I was a goner.

"That's one of our new blends. It's a sweet red, but it's not too sweet," she explained.

"What's it called?" Bridget asked.

Anna wrinkled her nose. "I'm not sure yet. Still thinking on that."

"That's my favorite too," I offered. See, I could be polite. I could actually stay on topic even though my body was a low hum of electricity solely due to Anna's presence.

"Why don't you name it Jasper's Red?" Simon mused. "I mean, you're a partner now, and you love it. It's a way to claim your stake."

Anna looked a little surprised, but then her pretty eyes widened. "That's a great idea," she finally said. "Jasper's Red. What do you think?" Her eyes landed on me.

I thought that felt too personal. I thought I was in over my head. A goat who shared my name, and now wine? I wanted to throttle Simon because I knew he was poking fun at me. I didn't, though. I simply shrugged. "If you think it's a good idea."

"Do you have a wine named after you?" Bridget queried, sipping her wine as she looked at Anna.

Anna shook her head quickly. "I don't. Haven't done that before."

"Well, maybe your next new wine should be named after you. You guys can have some kind of celebratory thing for your partnership," Simon offered.

Did I mention yet I wanted to throttle him? What the hell was he doing?

When Bridget said something to Anna, I cast a quick glare at Simon. He winked and took a swallow of his wine.

———

That night, after Simon and Bridget had left to go check into the bed and breakfast, I leaned my elbows on the counter in the upstairs loft apartment. Anna was jotting notes down for menu planning. "You don't have to name a wine after me, or yourself, for that matter. Simon was teasing."

"I know," Anna said. "Naming wines isn't my strong suit. Maybe when you decide what you want to do, you can let me know."

I lost track of the direction of the conversation because I didn't follow her detour. "Pardon?" I prompted.

"It doesn't make sense to name a wine after you if you're going to sell your half.

Once you decide, then we'll figure that out," she said.

Although her tone was matter-of-fact, I could see the worry swirling in her eyes and the subtle tension in her shoulders.

I needed a plan. And fast.

Because I was alone with Anna again, I was torn between two impulses. To fuck her or pull her in my arms and comfort her because I knew she was worried and felt like she was in over her head.

"Jasper?" Anna prompted.

"I haven't decided," I replied. Then I did something kind of cowardly. "You know it's your call."

She set her pencil on the counter. She'd been writing up another menu for the next wine tasting event. "You say that, but I know you really don't want to be a part of this." She looked down at the piece of paper, tracing her finger along the edge of the counter. When her eyes came up again, uncertainty flickered there. "We need to stop." Her cheeks went bright pink.

"Stop what?" I pressed, even though I knew exactly what she was talking about.

She licked her lips, and the urge to kiss her was so strong I almost gave in.

"We can't keep fooling around," she clarified.

I didn't know why I was feeling contrary, but I was. Just hearing her set that boundary notched the need racing through me even tighter.

"Fooling around? Is that what you call it? I beg to differ."

Standing opposite her while leaning my hands on the counter, I held her eyes. She didn't look away, but then I sensed she had a stubborn streak that rivaled mine and was never one to back down from a dare. I was daring her to look away.

"What do you mean?" she countered, her voice coming out a little raspy.

"Fooling around doesn't capture it. We're a blazing fire together, love. You know it," I said flatly.

Anna's cheeks flushed an even deeper shade of pink as we stared at each other. It felt as if lightning cracked through the air around us.

"It doesn't make it smart," she whispered. "I'm not like you. I can't—" She gestured vaguely with her hand in the air. "I need to think clearly, and I can't be casual about things like that."

I suddenly realized I was pushing too

hard. I dropped my hands and dipped my chin. "You're right. It definitely isn't smart."

Her eyes dropped to the counter, and she picked up her pencil. "I need to finish working on these."

Chapter Twenty-Six

ANNA

"How long will you be gone?" I asked Aubrey.

"Two weeks. Are you sure you don't mind?"

Pixy was frolicking in the paddock with Jasper and Tinker Bell. "Of course not. He's a good boy," I replied.

Aubrey grinned. "As good as a goat can be."

At that moment, Jasper turned into the parking area. He waved at us after he climbed out of his car and crossed the parking lot into the winery. Aubrey looked back toward me. "Jasper is nice. What exactly is the situation with him?"

I kept my sigh to myself, though I quickly summarized the situation, ending with, "...

and his grandfather's will requires him to stay here for a month and for me to agree in writing before he can sell."

Aubrey's brows hitched up. "That's a little unusual. How do you feel about it? I know you've been stressed about money."

"I don't know how I feel. I really don't want him to sell, but then I don't want to be stuck in a partnership with him if he doesn't want to be a part of it. It was so much easier with his grandfather. He just stayed over there and sent me friendly emails."

"Yeah, that's different from a hot British guy who's totally got eyes for you," she teased with a slow smile.

I opened my mouth to dispute that point but realized it was silly. My cheeks were hot when I shrugged. "I don't need to make it more complicated."

Aubrey's gaze was assessing as she looked at me. "He seems like a nice guy."

"I don't do flings very well," I finally said.

"Who said it has to be a fling?" she countered swiftly.

Crossing my arms, I rolled my eyes. "Just because Chance is head over heels in love with you doesn't mean that's what happens for everybody."

Aubrey knew my hit or miss luck with

men. It was nothing awful or heartbreaking, but I sure knew how to make not-so-great choices. I hated the whole online dating scene, which appeared to be the only way to meet anyone these days.

She gave me a hard eye roll in return. "There's nothing wrong with being optimistic. Chance and I didn't find our way to each other easily. You never know what could happen."

Jasper came out of the winery again, and blessedly, Aubrey dropped that topic. After she left, I went out to the greenhouse. I was in there checking on some seedlings when I heard the door open and close and glanced over to see Jasper. His eyes traveled around the space curiously. It always felt as if he was measuring and taking everything in. And I always felt as if everything came up short.

As if to prove my point, he crossed over to a shelf that was currently empty of any plants. "What happened here?" he asked as he leaned over to look under the table, eyeing the bucket there.

"The drainage system broke. I just haven't had time to fix it," I said, striving to keep my tone nonchalant. It was just one tray and not a big deal, but I'd been scrambling to keep up with everything and untangle the financial mess before he arrived. I felt defensive for myself and for my grandmother.

He studied it for a moment before straightening and turning to look at me. "I'll fix it. I'll pick up some parts at the hardware store."

"You don't have to. I'll get to it when—"

Jasper gave me a long look as one of his brows arched up slowly. I hated when he did that because it seemed so imperial.

"Anna, I can fix it. It's no big deal."

"Right. No big deal. That'd be great, thanks," I managed. I returned my focus to the seedlings, pointlessly tapping the soil around them.

"Are we not talking now?" Jasper pressed.

I hated that his British accent was both sexy and annoying. The conversation only flustered me and tipped me further off balance.

I cleared my throat. "We're talking right now, aren't we?"

"I suppose we are. Simon and Bridget would like to have dinner. They invited both of us."

"Oh." I pulled off my gardening gloves and turned, wiping my hands on my apron.

"Would you like to go?"

I knew there was no great way to avoid

dinner with them without appearing rude. "Of course. Tonight?"

Jasper nodded. My nipples tightened when I felt his gaze skim downward. For God's sake, my stupid nipples. They appeared to have a mind of their own and liked his attention. To make matters worse, the moment they tightened, I remembered the feel of his teeth grazing over them. The mere recollection of the sensation sent a little zing to my core.

His eyes came back up to mine, a subtle gleam in them. "I never knew overalls were a thing," he drawled in his crisp accent.

My mouth went dry as my belly shimmied. I had to lick my lips before I could even reply. "A thing?"

"You know, some men have a thing for shoes or tight skirts. Apparently, for me, it's overalls."

I felt hot all over, and my knees went a little wobbly. With that statement, he turned and left the greenhouse. I let out a sigh as I leaned my hips against the table. Reaching over, I turned on the faucet in the sink beside me and ran my hand under it, tossing the cold water on my face.

JASPER

"Oh, fucking admit it," Simon teased.

"Fucking admit what?" I countered.

We were eating dinner at a lovely restaurant with one of those staggering views along the Pacific Highway. The sun was slipping down toward the horizon above the ocean, with the sky stained faded red, gold, and tangerine. Bridget and Anna were away from the table at the dessert bar.

Simon knocked back the rest of his beer and set the bottle on the table. "You have a thing for Anna. She's absolutely charming."

I almost growled at Simon but caught myself in the nick of time. We'd spent a lot of time together during family visits growing up.

He knew all my buttons, and anything to do with Anna was apparently a new button.

"Fine, she is lovely. It doesn't matter if I have a thing for her. She doesn't think it's smart."

I left the rest unspoken. I wasn't about to say out loud that my two encounters with Anna would probably stand the test of time as the hottest sexual encounters of my life.

Simon's sharp gaze assessed me. "It isn't smart if you're just using her, but I think you really like her. Don't wait too long to be smarter than me."

"Pardon?"

"It took me a little longer than I'd like to come to terms with how I felt about Bridget, and we lost some time. When it's that good, every minute counts."

"For fuck's sake, Simon. I *do* like her, and I don't want to use her, but you and Bridget are madly in love and committed. I'm not sure I'm there yet."

Simon shrugged lightly, casting me a knowing look as if he knew some secret I didn't. Anna and Bridget returned to the table with a selection of desserts, putting an effective end to that uncomfortable conversation.

Just to torture me, when we were departing in the parking lot, Simon smiled over at Anna. "It's been absolutely lovely to meet you. Next time Jasper comes to visit us in New York, you should come with him. Have you ever been to the East Coast?"

Anna shook her head. "Actually, I haven't. That might be nice. I'll see you again before you go, right?"

"Of course. We have a few more days," Bridget chimed in.

We said our goodbyes, and with a warm smile, Anna waved at them as I drove away and silently cursed Simon.

Chapter Twenty-Eight

ANNA

Days passed until Jasper only had a week and a half left before he completed his month here at the winery. I tried to stay busy. Well, I didn't have to try. I was busy no matter what. It was impossible not to be, which was a blessed relief.

Although it made perfect sense because I needed to not be stupid, it wasn't easy to maintain that boundary I'd set with Jasper. That old lesson most of us learned in kindergarten about keeping our hands to ourselves took on new meaning. You try living with a sexy British guy whose occasional teasing smile broke through his grumpy attitude, and whose hot bod was hard to ignore.

He was very respectful and kept his distance. Except his eyes could set me on fire with nothing more than a passing look. The air often felt as if lightning were about to strike, filled with heavy tension as desire stormed through me.

One evening, I busied myself in the winery after Eloise went home, sterilizing wine bottles to use for small gifts for people who came to our next scheduled tasting. It was late, but then I'd been working late every night. It was better than finding myself alone with Jasper upstairs in the small loft apartment.

Everything was going fine. It wasn't like I had to think much about this process because I'd done it hundreds of times. But then two things happened at once. My phone rang, and the winery phone rang. We still had this old phone mounted on the wall, and its ring was enough to shatter your nerves.

Startled at the sound, I jumped and dropped a bottle in my hands. I didn't know what I did wrong next, but in the process of trying to clean up the broken glass, I ended up with a giant gash on one hand, so deep that my knees collapsed and nausea welled when I saw it.

I didn't know how long I sat there on the cold tile floor before Jasper appeared in the doorway. I'd grabbed a towel and wrapped it around my mangled hand. He was across the room in a second, kneeling beside me. "What happened, Anna?" he prompted.

I felt a little lightheaded as I looked up into his concerned eyes. I swallowed. "I dropped a bottle and cut my hand," I said slowly.

Jasper was all business although concern emanated from him. He efficiently took the hand I was cradling and unwrapped the towel. It was stained with my bright red blood. When I looked down, I felt lightheaded again, almost as if I were falling, so I was relieved I was already sitting on the floor.

"You need stitches," he announced.

I started to shake my head, but he gave me a stern look. "We're not arguing about this, Anna."

"I don't have health insurance. I can't afford it," I blurted out.

"Fucking America, and their stupid health insurance system," Jasper muttered. "I'll pay for the bill. You need stitches," he repeated.

I didn't have it in me to argue. The next hour or so passed in a blur. Jasper got me into his rental car, instead of my old junker. Somehow, he even found the closest walk-in clinic without any guidance from me. My hand was throbbing, and it was still bleeding. Even the fresh towel wrapped around it was stained deep red with blood by the time we got to the clinic. It turned out, Jasper was bossy. He had me situated in a small examination room with a kind doctor in a matter of minutes.

"Now," she began, "would you like your husband to stay or go while I stitch you up?"

I looked from her to Jasper, who was kind of glaring at her.

"It's fine if he stays," I finally said, not really having it in me to correct her impression that he was my husband.

She had my hand stitched up quickly and was discussing the three days of painkillers she planned to give me and how to clean it with Jasper. I was suddenly exhausted and just wanted to go to bed.

Jasper excused himself to use the restroom. The doctor, Dr. Janet as she had introduced herself, looked over at me. "Your husband sure is protective and worried about you. You found yourself a good man," she said, her cheeks plumping with her smile as her blue eyes twinkled.

I knew he was a good catch, but he wasn't mine. I finally felt the need to correct her. "He's not actually my husband."

She had turned her attention to the computer and glanced up quickly. "Perhaps not, but I can assure you he really likes you."

———

...he really likes you.

The doctor's words kept dashing through my thoughts. Was it that obvious? I didn't doubt Jasper wanted me sexually, but he liked me? I found that *really* hard to believe.

When we returned to the winery, Jasper practically carried me up the stairs. I had to swat him away with my good hand and thanked the stars I hadn't injured my right hand.

"I can walk up the stairs," I protested.

He kind of glowered at me. "Fine. I'm right here if you need me."

We got up to the loft, and I turned to him. "It's just a cut, you know. I'm fine." I lifted my hand as if to prove my point.

"Tomorrow, don't even think about dealing with the chickens or the goats. Or anything, for that matter. I'll take care of it," was his reply.

My mouth must have fallen open then because Jasper let out a growly kind of sigh. "What? You know I can deal with the goats and the chickens. I've helped you a number of times. I will also handle the wine tasting."

My cheeks got hot. "Jasper, I can handle the wine tasting. I'll let you take care of the goat and chicken feedings."

He shook his head sharply. "You can sit at the bar during the wine tasting and chat with customers. But you don't need to work."

We were still standing by the doorway. Annoyed, I turned away and toed off my tennis shoes. Crossing into the kitchen, I was startled when he appeared by my side rapidly. "What do you need?" he asked.

"Something to drink," I said slowly, giving him a weird look because he was being totally weird.

"You can't have alcohol," he announced as if he had some sort of say in the matter.

He opened the refrigerator, his eyes scanning the contents. "Take your pick, cranberry juice, lemonade, or water." When he looked up, his gaze was completely serious. He seemed to have no idea how ridiculous he was being.

I burst out laughing. "For starters, I can have wine if I want."

He didn't laugh. His eyes swept over me, lingering on my hand. Which, come to think of it, was throbbing. The painkillers they'd given me at the walk-in clinic hadn't kicked in yet, and the local anesthetic they'd sprayed over it for the stitching was clearly wearing off.

"The doctor said you can't drink with the painkiller she prescribed," he said kind of sternly.

"Oh, for God's sake," I muttered. "I don't want wine. I was just making a point. I'll take some water, please."

With that, I turned and actually flounced over to the couch. I was irritable and annoyed. Now, I had to deal with this hand thing. I didn't have time. Speaking of things I didn't have, I recalled that I didn't have health insurance again. I *really* didn't want Jasper covering my medical bill.

When he crossed the room with a glass of water and set it beside me on the table, he sat down at an angle on the opposite end of the sectional, giving me a considering look. I took a swallow of water before looking over at him. "You're not covering my medical bill," I announced, trying to inject a firm tone into my words.

"I already did," he replied with a dispassionate and definitely firm tone.

What was I doing thinking about firm things? I knew what I wanted. Jasper firm in my hands, and Jasper firm over me. He was *firm* in many places.

I suddenly got hot and realized I was starting to feel a little loopy. "Fine, but only this time." I aimed for casual nonchalance.

"The health care situation in this country is barbaric," he added.

"Tell me something I don't know as someone who has no health insurance because it's too expensive." I rolled my eyes and reached for the glass of water again. This time, I almost dropped it.

He was over there so fast, I didn't even notice him until he was right beside me lifting the water glass from my hand. "Pain meds kicking in?" he asked.

I finished a swallow of water, and he returned the glass to the table. "I guess so." I leaned back in the couch.

"I'm going to add health insurance to the business budget tomorrow." Moving the water glass out of my reach, he sat down again, this time only about a foot away from me.

The last thing I remembered was looking over at Jasper and telling him, "You're too handsome. It's annoying."

An indeterminate amount of time later, I woke up in my bed. For a moment, I was confused because I didn't remember getting in bed. Then I rolled over and realized my hand was really sore.

Most of the night came rushing back—dropping the bottle, trying to clean up in a rush, and cutting myself. Then Jasper being all worried and bossy and grumpy. The pain meds must've knocked me out because I didn't remember getting from the couch to my bed.

I gently lifted my hand. It was sore, but I could deal with it. When I sat up in bed, I realized I smelled Jasper. Looking down, I discovered I was wearing one of his T-shirts. There was nothing distinctive about it, and it swallowed me whole and smelled like him. I shamelessly curled my good hand in the fabric and lifted it for a nice long breath in. God. Even his shirt smelled so good it turned me on. I didn't know what kind of laundry soap he used, but his shirt carried a crisp, clean scent with a hint of him—whatever *him* was—underneath.

The wooden floor was cool under my feet when I rested them on it to stand. The T-shirt fell to my knees, so I decided it was safe to venture out into the main area. Because I needed to pee. A girl's got to take care of her needs first.

There was no sign of Jasper when I tip-toed out and slipped into the bathroom. After taking care of matters and gently washing my hands, being careful not to get any water on the bandage right along the edge of my palm, I brushed my teeth and then ventured back to the living room.

Jasper was at the kitchen counter wearing a pair of sweatpants and no shirt. My hormones stood up and did a little cheer inside my body. My God, he had a great ass. The way the sweatpants curved over that muscular surface had me itching to reach over and stroke a palm over it.

He turned, and my mouth practically watered at the sight of his chest—all muscled planes, with that smattering of dark hair that narrowed to a very well-defined happy trail. He reached behind him without even turning and tapped the button to turn on the coffee maker.

"How do you feel?" he asked as he crossed over to me, oblivious to the fact he was sending my hormones into overdrive. It had nothing to do with anything other than wanting to jump him. The sexy kind of jump, that is.

"Fine," I squeaked. "Did you help me get

in bed last night?" I fingered the hem of his T-shirt.

He studied me quietly before nodding slowly. "Yes. If carrying you to your bed and getting you changed after you told me you refused to sleep in your clothes counts as help."

"I think it counts as help," I managed in return, uncomfortable with how close he was. I took a step back and crossed over to look out the windows.

The sun was just cresting the horizon. Rays of gold stretched into the sky, mingling with the fading oranges and reds of the sunrise. Dew glimmered on the flowers and the fields in the distance. The landscape sparkled.

"How do you feel?" Jasper repeated as he came to stand beside me.

"Fine," I said. "I don't need any more painkillers. Ibuprofen should do the trick."

"I'll get you some."

Chapter Twenty-Nine

JASPER

I handed Anna two ibuprofen. She popped them in her mouth, and I passed over a glass of water, taking it from her the moment she lowered it from her lips.

When she swiped her pink tongue across her bottom lip, catching a drop of water, it felt as if a bolt of lightning struck my body. Bloody hell. She was injured, so I did *not* need to be lusting after her now.

I turned away abruptly and crossed the room to set the glass of water by the sink. When I turned back, Anna was walking to meet me. I didn't know what to think of how fucking sexy I thought she was in my T-shirt. I'd only put it on her out of desperate self-preservation last night.

She'd fallen asleep on the couch, so I carried her to bed. She'd tested every ounce of discipline I had when she came awake. When I lowered her to bed, she tried to pull me in with her. Then it got even worse.

She sat up. "I can't sleep with this on." She'd yanked at her shirt. "Men don't understand how uncomfortable it is to fall asleep in a bra," she'd then offered up as a deep philosophical point. "This is serious."

I'd literally had to grit my teeth to help her out of her shirt and bra. While I'd turned away to drape them on a chair near her bed, she'd started shimmying out of her jeans. Considering she got one leg out and the other stuck, I had no choice but to help her, but then she was practically naked. Out of sheer desperation, I'd yanked off my own T-shirt and put it on her before tucking her under the covers.

Needing to get my mind off that vision, I said, "I've already fed the goats and the chickens."

"Without your shirt on?" she countered, her cheeks flushing slightly at that.

"I had a shirt on, but I got some chicken shit on it, so I put it in the hamper and showered," I explained.

Anna caught the corner of her lip in her

teeth, worrying it a little and making me want to kiss her. I shouldn't have known exactly how many days had passed since I had her sweet lips underneath mine. If you were wondering, it was six. Six days too many.

"Thank you for helping out," she said quietly.

"You're welcome. I really don't mind. Jasper is growing on me," I offered with a chuckle, thinking of how the little goat had greeted me with a head butt in the calves this morning.

Anna smiled and walked back toward the counter. Like the fool I was for her, I followed, stopping a few feet away from her. I wasn't feeling rational, not in the slightest. In fact, I'd been a little bit crazy since I found her last night with her bloodied hand.

Continuing my tendency not to think, I took one stride, closing the distance between us. Lifting a hand, I brushed a wayward lock of hair off her cheek and tucked it behind her ear.

She shivered slightly, and her cheeks went pink again. "You're not allowed to work too much until that's better," I heard myself saying.

"Jasper," she began.

I shook my head. "Don't boss me, Anna."

Her pretty brown eyes narrowed, and her teeth released her bottom lip. "How about you don't boss me?" she countered.

When she took a breath, her breasts brushed against my chest, and I could feel the tight points of her nipples through the cotton of my T-shirt. It didn't help matters for the state of my body that I knew she only had on a pair of panties under there, if that.

She felt almost dangerous to me. She was certainly dangerous to my sanity and shredded my control with no effort whatsoever. I rested my hands on either side of her hips on the counter behind her as if somehow that would help me get a grip.

"Have you decided what you want to do?" she asked, her voice falling into the weighted space surrounding us.

The air felt as if it had been lit with a charge, but I answered her with the truth. "I don't want to sell."

Her eyes searched mine, almost as if she couldn't believe it. I shrugged. "I think my grandfather would've liked me to choose not to do that."

While that *was* true, that wasn't why I'd come to my conclusion. Oh no. That was all Anna. I knew how much this place meant to her, and I knew that if she took what little money she had after she bought me out, she would still be scrambling to get back onto solid footing. Not changing the arrangement would make it possible for her to truly re-coup the losses her grandmother had incurred.

"Oh," she finally said. "Really?"

I nodded slowly, trying to think over the echoing beat of my heart and the need twisting like flames through my veins. "I have one request."

"What's that?" she whispered.

"I want to kiss you."

Her breath hitched in the back of her throat, and the sound shot like fire through my body. I didn't realize I was holding my breath until she spoke again, and I finally let it out.

"If I don't kiss you, will you change your mind and want to sell?"

I shook my head. I wasn't going to lie to her, even if I wanted the leverage it might give me.

Her eyes widened, and her nostrils flared. "I don't know if I can stop at a kiss," she said, and I almost groaned at the raw honesty in her words and in her eyes.

"That's up to you."

She bit her lip and shifted her legs. I

knew she was rubbing her thighs together, and I knew what that meant.

I forced myself, by scrambling together what little discipline I had, to wait. I needed to know she really wanted this.

"Okay," she finally whispered.

My body sent up a silent hallelujah, but I still waited, curling my fingers around the edge of the counter as if the counter itself could keep me sane in the force of desire roaring through my body like wind across a flat landscape with nothing to slow it down.

"Okay, what?" I said carefully.

"Okay, kiss me."

"Just a kiss?" I pressed, my fingers tightening even further on the counter.

She bit her lip and shifted her thighs again. "No. Don't stop there. That would be mean."

Then she inched closer, placing one hand on my chest. My heart lurched toward her palm as she slid her other hand up around the back of my neck and pulled me down to kiss her.

In a hot second, I was delving into the warm sweetness of Anna's mouth. She tasted minty. When she sighed and flexed into me, I slid my hand down to cup her sweet bottom, savoring the little whimper she made in my mouth. I rocked my arousal into the cradle of her hips.

I abruptly recalled she had an injured hand and tore my lips from hers as I took in a gulp of air. "Be careful," I managed to say.

"Of you?" she countered, looking a little surprised.

"Of your hand," I murmured as I glanced down at where it rested on my chest.

"My hand is fine. I promise, this won't hurt it," she said with a sly, saucy grin. I was distracted a little by that, but I made a mental note not to forget about her hand.

"Here," I said. I lifted her and slipped her hips onto the counter, promptly discovering it was the perfect height.

My T-shirt slid up on her thighs, revealing those purple cotton panties I'd had to blank out of my mind last night. They were cute with a little cotton bow right in the front.

Dipping my head into the side of her neck, I breathed in her sweet, musky scent before I pressed hot open kisses along there, letting out a growl of satisfaction on her skin. She shivered and arched toward me.

I tugged her hips a little closer to the edge of the counter, savoring the feel of her hot core against my swollen arousal. We didn't have much between us, what with my thin cotton sweatpants and her panties, yet I felt all *too* much.

With a yank, I sent my T-shirt flying off her and caught one breast with my palm, savoring its silky weight right before I dipped my head and swirled my tongue around her dusky pink nipple.

Fuck me. I loved how responsive Anna was. She let out something between a sigh and whimper before her fingers slid into my hair—her good hand, mind you—and she murmured my name in a breathy gasp.

She arched into my mouth as I slid a palm down over the curve of her belly, teasing into her trimmed curls as I pushed her panties out of the way. My fingers were slick with her arousal when I delved into her folds. She let out a sharp cry when I sank two fingers into her, knuckle deep.

I *needed* to taste her. After a light nip on her nipple, I leaned down and pushed her knees apart. Her pussy was so wet the cotton was drenched.

"These are in the way," I muttered as I hooked a hand over the elastic and lifted her hips to yank them down quickly. "There we go." I pushed her knees apart and glanced down. Her pussy was swollen and glistening. I teased my fingers over her again, watching as her eyes fell closed and her breasts rose and fell as she took sharp pants.

I blew lightly on her sex, satisfaction rolling through me when her hips arched, and she trembled slightly. I wanted to slow this down, but nothing was ever slow with Anna. I felt as if something had caught me in its current, a riptide of need and a fierce desire to claim her.

I looked just as I buried my fingers inside her again. She shuddered, her channel convulsing around my fingers. I dragged my tongue through her slick arousal. She tasted salty and sweet. The sound of her gasping my name between ragged breaths only made my cock swell to the point of pain.

Keeping in tune with our tendency to rush through everything, she was climaxing in a noisy burst in a matter of seconds. "Jasper," she gasped as I straightened.

"Yes?" I reached for my cock, shoving my sweatpants down and kicking them free so fast it was a miracle I didn't fall over.

"I need you," she murmured.

I had my cock in my fist and was just about to sink inside her when I realized I needed a condom. I started to draw back, but she was strong, injured hand notwithstanding. She curled her legs around me and held tight. "Where are you going?" she demanded.

"Condom," I bit out.

"I have an IUD, and I promise I'm clean. I actually don't remember the last time I had sex before you." She cocked her head to the side then as if she were going to try to figure this out now.

"I've never had sex without a condom."

"Never?"

I shook my head. "I've always been careful."

"Well, in that case, if you insist," she said, loosening her legs.

The thing was, I trusted her completely. Now that I knew I could be inside her without a single thing between us, well, I didn't think I could resist.

"No need to insist."

When I felt the first kiss of her arousal on my thick crown, I groaned. My forehead fell to hers, and I sank home inside her slowly. Inch by intoxicating inch, she sheathed me in her silky clench.

When I was buried deep, I held still, scrambling to gain some control. "Sweetheart," I murmured against her lips. "You feel so fucking good." My words were slurred, and I felt drugged and dragged into the most intense pleasure I'd ever experienced.

She let out this whispered gasp, saying something unintelligible. When I felt her hand fall to my chest and the subtle brush of her bandage on me, I reminded myself I could only fuck her so hard.

But Anna had this way of making me forget everything. When she rocked her hips into me as I gripped her with my palm, right at the base of her spine with my fingers splayed over one of her sweet ass cheeks, I was gone. I sank into her satiny heat again and again. She slowly dropped her legs, and that movement created the friction she was after. The moment her legs fell, she was crying out, and I felt her rippling around me. Electricity sizzled through me, and my balls tightened. She cried out, her fingers pressing against my chest when she threw her head back and gasped my name.

My own release slammed into me, that riptide dragging me under before it curled and threw me back on the shore. I came in rough shudders as I held on tight to her.

Awareness came in fragments—the feel of her breasts against my chest, her palm sliding over my shoulder, the subtle brush of her bandage on my skin, my breath gradually slowing, and the sound of my own blood rushing in my ears with every thundering beat of my heart.

I eventually lifted my head, almost afraid to look in her eyes, but I managed. Wide and brown, they searched my face.

I startled myself with what I said next. "Are you going to tell me we can't do that again? Because you've ruined me."

She watched me quietly before shaking her head just barely. "No. It might not be smart, but it feels too good."

Chapter Thirty

ANNA

Following Jasper's orders that night, I didn't really work. We had our weekly wine tasting, and we had quite a crowd. It appeared that word had traveled that a sexy British man was now co-owner of the winery. He was quite the draw.

Jasper had enlisted Eloise's help for the night with a few other staff. He stayed behind the bar and chatted it up with customers. I sat on a stool nearby with my feet hooked over the rungs, thinking I couldn't wait until the night ended. Because I wanted more of Jasper. As I'd told him this morning, it felt too good.

"How are you holding up?"

I'd been staring off into space and glanced

in his direction at the question. "Fine," I insisted. "It's not that bad. It's just my hand. And if you weren't here, I'd be handling everything fine."

His sharp gaze coasted over me, and it felt like fire on my skin everywhere his gaze landed. When his eyes made their way back to mine, he lowered his chin slightly. "I know you would. But it's not necessary. While it is just your hand, you did need stitches. Eight to be exact."

"You counted?"

He flashed a grin then. "I did."

At that moment, a woman called, "I'd love to try a few wines."

She was already tipsy, so I knew she'd already tried the wines several times. Jasper turned, ever solicitous, and went over to help her. I didn't miss the way she batted her eyelashes and gave him a coquettish smile.

"Jasper likes you," Eloise said from my side.

Heat flared on my cheeks, but I ignored it and shrugged. "You really think so? He's just being nice because I hurt myself last night."

"You *do* know the sound travels from the loft, right?" she teased with a sly smile.

"Busted," Eloise added when I winced.

"Oh my God," I muttered as I grabbed my glass of wine with my good hand and took a long swallow.

"He sounds talented," she offered.

"Please stop," I pleaded.

She winked. "That's all you'll hear from me about it. You need something to help you relax, and I think Jasper is a great plan for that."

Later that night, after Jasper insisted on cleaning everything up with my oversight, we went back up to the loft apartment. Looking his way, I said, "We might've been overheard this morning."

"Might've been?" he returned with a chuckle. "Eloise told me I'd better keep up the good work."

I should've taken this as a warning to pump the brakes on this madness. But I was foolish, so I didn't.

I dove headfirst into what I knew would be a brief but hot affair with Jasper. It was the opposite of smart. It was colossally stupid, and I couldn't stop myself.

Chapter Thirty-One

JASPER

"That was amazing," Bridget said as she set her fork down and pushed her plate back.

Anna smiled over at her, her cheeks pinkening slightly. "Thanks. I'm glad you two could come for brunch before you left."

Simon and Bridget had stopped by for brunch with us before they headed to the airport. Anna had insisted on cooking for them. The meal consisted of fluffy scrambled eggs with fresh tomatoes, goat cheese, and fresh herbs from the garden, along with bacon and roasted potatoes.

I knew when I flew back to London, I would miss the food. As if reading my mind, Simon caught my eyes. "Does Anna cook like this for you every day?" he teased.

I shrugged. "Almost. But I don't insist."

Anna took a swallow of her coffee. "How long is your flight?" she asked, shifting the topic.

"Almost eight hours," Bridget said. "Fortunately, it's a direct flight."

"How much longer are you staying here?" Simon asked me.

I shifted my shoulders slightly, hoping Simon didn't pick up on my discomfort. I didn't particularly want to discuss this. "I'm scheduled to leave next week."

He nodded and didn't say anything further. Bridget, however, did. "Have you decided what you're going to do?"

"About what?"

"The business," she clarified with an encouraging smile.

"I'm not selling."

I snuck a quick look at Anna, noticing the twitch of worry between her brows. She never said it, but I sensed she was waiting for me to change my mind. I wasn't going to, and I didn't enjoy contemplating my subtle emotional uneasiness about why.

"Smart move," Simon chimed in.

"Oh, good to know you think it's smart," I teased lightly.

Simon rolled his eyes. "It is smart. I'm

not just saying that to be nice. Plus, I think your grandfather would've liked your choice."

"His ridiculous requirements in the will made it clear to me that he didn't want me to sell. It's also a solid investment," I explained.

All of this was entirely true, however that wasn't why I wasn't selling. The sense of protectiveness I felt toward Anna was too powerful to ignore. I knew she loved this place and couldn't imagine her having to give it up.

There was a light knock on the door at the back of the winery kitchen where we were eating. Anna stood, peering out the windows. "Oh, I forgot. One of my grandmother's old friends is stopping by to pick up some perennials. I'll be back in a few."

She hurried out, leaving me behind with Simon and Bridget. Bridget looked at me, her eyes asscssing. "You really like Anna," she observed.

The tension in my neck and shoulders tightened slightly. "Of course, I like Anna," I replied, striving to keep my tone casual. I wasn't about to mention that every time I let myself think about Anna, my heart thrashed in my chest. I also wasn't about to mention that keeping my hands off her would take an act of God at this point, or so it felt. And I didn't consider myself a religious man.

Ever since last week, the day after she'd hurt her hand, I'd felt as if I were running too fast downhill. I couldn't stop for fear of tripping and falling. The momentum of my emotions and need propelled me forward. Not a night had passed when we didn't fall asleep tangled up together since.

It felt good, dangerously good. Yet it was stupid. Really stupid. Anna herself had said it wasn't smart, but I'd arrogantly thought I could control it and keep it compartmentalized.

Simon drained his coffee and cocked his head to the side. He regarded me quietly before his eyes slid to Bridget's. "Of course, he likes her. He doesn't have enough sense to do the right thing about it yet."

"What the hell are you talking about?" I muttered.

"You're going to leave," he said flatly.

"Obviously, I'm going to leave. I need to go home and run a business." I hoped my irritation didn't show in my voice.

"You can run your business from wherever you want," Simon retorted smoothly.

Anna returned with a streak of dirt on her cheek, and my heart thudded restlessly in my chest when she stopped beside the table. "Do you all need anything else?"

Bridget smiled up at her. "Of course not. You don't need to wait on us."

Anna shrugged and automatically began picking up the empty plates. Bridget stood to help her, and Simon lingered at the table for another moment.

"What?" I asked when he looked from Anna to me.

"Maybe ask yourself why you're so irritable," he said lightly.

Not much later, I stood beside Anna in the parking lot and waved as Simon and Bridget drove away. I wasn't paying attention when Jasper came up and head butted me in the back of my legs. I stumbled slightly and looked down at him. "Really, dude? I thought we were friends."

Anna laughed. "He is your friend. That's why he's doing that."

Looking up at her, I narrowed my eyes. "That doesn't make sense. He head butted me the very first time he saw me."

She threw her head back with a laugh. "Maybe so," she said, her brown eyes twinkling as she looked over at me. "But now, he really does like you."

Eloise called for Anna from the winery kitchen, and the day swept into busy-ness.

I intended to try to have something like a

conversation with Anna later that day, but I never got the chance. I did, however, find it impossible to resist her that night. I found myself in the shower with her, admiring just how amazing the soap bubbles looked on her skin.

Chapter Thirty-Two

ANNA

"Jasper!" I gasped impatiently.

He lifted me easily, but then, he was that kind of guy. Strong enough that with an assist from the tiled shower wall, he could lift me in his arms and sink inside me. Just like that, I was full of Jasper.

I was awash in pleasure, and I was still being stupid about it. It was almost annoying how good we were together. Jasper was a generous lover and spoiled me.

When I fell asleep later, I told myself he was leaving soon. I reminded myself life would go back to the way it was before. Except now I didn't have to worry so much about money. I might miss Jasper for a little bit, but it would pass. It *had* to pass. Right?

Those days flew by in a blur, and suddenly, I woke up and looked at the calendar. Today was the day Jasper would drive away. I hated goodbyes, like *really* hated them.

I didn't have to try to stay busy to keep myself distracted because there was always more than enough to do. I even made sure I was tied up with customers when it was time for him to leave. Eloise appeared in the front area of the winery.

"I'm covering," she said sternly, arching her silver brows and sort of glaring at me.

"I've got it," I said lightly.

"You're needed in the back," she returned pointedly and practically shoved me through the door into the kitchen.

The very second I saw Jasper standing by the door across the room, my heart started rioting in my chest and I felt a little sick. He wasn't wearing a suit today although he did have on slacks and a rich blue button-down shirt. It set off his eyes, and he looked delectable. He made a habit of looking delectable with no effort whatsoever.

Don't be a coward, you can handle a goodbye.

Crossing the room, I stopped in front of him. "Are you going?" I asked the most obvious question possible at the moment.

I prayed he would make this quick. Because I'd gone and fallen for Jasper. I needed him to go so I could get started with getting over him.

"I thought perhaps you weren't going to let me say goodbye," he said, his tone somber.

My throat was tight, but I managed a quick breath. I swallowed, praying that I didn't cry. "Just busy," I squeaked. Looking down at the floor, I added, "Thank you for your help."

When I looked back into his eyes, I felt compelled to say what came next. "If you change your mind and want to sell, I'll sign the agreement." Those words came out in a rush.

He was still quiet. I worried my heart was pounding so loud even he could hear it. After a moment, he finally spoke, "I'm not going to change my mind, Anna."

"Okay." I took a step back, but he was faster than me and caught my good hand in his, reeling me close

"One more kiss."

"I hate goodbyes," I whispered.

"I hate saying goodbye to you," he whispered in return, just before brushing his lips over mine and pulling me close.

———

Jasper left. That night when I went up to the loft, it felt so empty. So empty that I called Aubrey and asked her if she'd bring me one of those kittens from the litter she found. She'd just told me about it the day before. Aubrey blessedly didn't ask why and showed up a little while later with an orange kitten.

"I think they're about ten weeks old. This one's a little girl. I even brought you some kitten food." She handed the kitten over, and the kitten immediately started purring.

"Thank you."

"You can call him, you know," she said pointedly before leaving.

I promptly named my new kitten Mango. She kept me thoroughly occupied with her sweetness and playfulness. I still missed Jasper, though, so much that every cell of my body carried an echoing ache.

Chapter Thirty-Three

JASPER

Three weeks later

"What now?" I snapped.

"Damn, you need to relax," Simon's voice came through the phone line.

I caught myself about to actually growl into the phone line. "Apologies. I thought you were my assistant."

"Is that how you talk to your assistant?" Simon countered.

This time, I had to catch myself before I sighed. "When I'm running late on a financial report, yes, I suppose I can be impatient."

"Ah, I see. When you're cranky, you're an ass to your staff. Not a good look."

"Hello, Simon. Shall we start again? How are you doing, and what can I do for you today?" I asked smoothly.

"Bridget wanted to know if you'd be coming back to the US soon, now that you have business interests here."

I didn't miss the sly sarcasm in my cousin's tone, and I knew without a doubt he was making no effort to disguise it. "No current plans," I quickly replied, trying to keep my tone neutral. I knew where this was going, and I was already annoyed.

"How is Anna?" he asked, his tone downright cheery now. I imagined he enjoyed making me uncomfortable. The only advantage I had was he couldn't actually see me.

"I wouldn't know. I haven't spoken to her."

"In three weeks?"

My heart gave a tricky twist in my chest, and my stomach felt a little hollow. I was being an asshole.

"I wasn't really paying attention to the time," I lied, blatantly. I knew exactly how many days it had been since I'd seen Anna. Twenty-two, in fact, one day past three weeks.

Simon was quiet and then let out a rather

elaborate sigh. "Really, Jasper? I thought maybe you finally met someone who would get you to think about something other than business and move beyond your parents' miserable marriage."

"Since when was I your personal project?"

"You're not my personal project. You're my cousin, and whether it's smart or not, I actually give a damn about you. You seemed more relaxed than I can ever recall when we visited you in California. As a fellow human with workaholic tendencies, I was happy for you. I'm guessing you brought yourself back to London and returned to a life of constant work."

"I had a lot to catch up on," I said, almost wincing at the defensive tone in my voice.

"Sure, you did," Simon replied. I could practically feel his disappointment emanating through the phone line into my ear.

"I did," I insisted, practically biting my tongue after that. Because my insistence only revealed I was trying to make a point, more to myself than Simon

"Obviously, I know you had plenty to catch up on, Jasper. You're generally a busy guy, as most of us are. You'll have to talk to Anna at some point, seeing as you own a business with her. Or I suppose you could delegate that to one of your minions."

"Simon," I warned.

"What? No one else will talk back to you, so I'm just trying to help. I'd like to see you a little happier and enjoying life more."

"How is Bridget?" I hoped that detour would get him off his focus on Anna.

It did for a little bit. We chatted like a regular catch-up phone call until the very end. We were saying goodbye when Simon said, "Call Anna. Don't be an ass."

———

My solicitor stared at me in surprise. "This is not what I expected," he finally said.

"What did you expect?" I growled.

I seemed to be growling a lot and snapping at people. I was in a constant state of irritation.

Benjamin, who'd known me for years, gave me a long look as he leaned back in his desk chair. "I expected you to want to sell. I figured a month would give you enough time to persuade Miss Lennon to agree to let you sell."

I wasn't about to share the fact that Anna told me she would agree to the sale.

"It's a good investment, if a bit unconventional."

He simply stared at me. "Okay, then."

That night, I walked into my flat. The sound of my keys dropping in the bowl on the table by the door echoed loudly. Compared to Anna's loft flat at the winery, my flat was gigantic, and the space felt empty and cold. Rain lashed the windows on this dreary London evening. Hell, I couldn't even call it evening. It was close to midnight.

I knew exactly what time it was in California, and I wanted to call Anna. She had nicely texted me the day of my trip to make sure I landed safely. I'd replied that I had.

I tapped open my phone, my eyes landing on our last text exchange. My heart gave an achy thump. I was being an ass, as Simon helpfully pointed out. He'd adopted some Americanisms since he'd met Bridget and now lived in the US full-time. Ass did have a little more punch to it than arse.

I finally gave in to the urge. I didn't call, but I texted.

How are you? Been thinking of you.

The urge to tell her that I missed her was strong, but I had some well-formed habits, and all of them involved dodging intimacy. It wasn't particularly hard *not* to tell her I missed her. However, not communicating the feeling didn't change it. Not in the slightest. I missed her fiercely.

———

I came awake with a start. I'd fallen asleep fully dressed on my couch. Disoriented, I glanced around, finally realizing the sound of my phone buzzing on the coffee table was what had punctured my sleep.

I grabbed it and scrubbed my hand over my face. I read Anna's return text with bleary eyes.

I'm well. I hope you are too. If you've reconsidered selling, please just let me know.

I wanted to throw the phone because her cold, stilted, and polite response was unsatisfactory. Nothing like the warm, willing girl I'd spent too many nights with and who I dreamt about every night since I'd left.

A few days later, in what I could only describe as a fit of pique with myself, I attempted to go on a date. Well, let me clarify. It wasn't a date. I had an arrangement with Jane, a colleague who worked as the CFO for another business. She was lovely and intelligent and had no expectations, none at all. She was too busy for romance and occasionally needed a date for business functions, and we occasionally attached benefits to that arrangement.

That evening, I was miserable, so miserable that Jane glanced my way. "What is wrong with you, Jasper? If I didn't know better, I'd say you were a fussy toddler."

"A fussy toddler?" I returned, affronted.

"Exactly. You've been irritable with everyone. What is wrong?"

We had a moment alone, and all I could do was shrug. "My apologies."

I got through the rest of the night, calling upon my manners to keep me polite. Just when I thought I was going to skate free, I glanced across the room and saw my parents.

The moment I laid eyes on them, anger flashed inside. My father was an asshole. He was flirting with another woman right in front of my mother. My mother's face was pinched, which led me to believe she was not currently also enjoying an affair. They made a mockery of the term marriage, always trying to one-up each other. I didn't think either one of them even understood the concept of love, though they certainly understood the concepts of jealousy and manufactured drama for the sake of it.

Yet here you are having dinner, planning to

take Jane home and go through the motions. She's a nice woman and can never be a substitute for Anna. Don't use her.

My fucking conscience took that moment to give me a mental kick. Bloody hell. I was starting to get tired of thinking about Anna, yet I could *not* stop. I found my feet moving, crossing over to my parents on the far side of the room.

My mother looked up and smiled tightly. "Hello, Jasper. I was wondering if we would see you here tonight," she said smoothly. As usual, she wore black and her dark hair was pulled back into a tight twist.

"Hello, Mother," I said, dipping my chin in acknowledgment. She leaned up and pressed a dry kiss to my cheek, the only form of affection I'd ever experienced from her that I could recall.

My father glanced over. "Hello," he said, his tone brusque. The woman beside him blinked at me with coquettish eyes.

I simply nodded. "I heard from Ben that you're keeping your stake in that winery," my father said as he stepped closer to my mother, all but dismissing the poor woman standing at his side. I could only feel so bad for her because she was openly flirting with a man right in front of his wife, but then... I sighed silently, cutting off that train of thought.

"I am," I replied. I preferred not to discuss business with my father.

He gave me a long look. "I heard about the unusual conditions of your grandfather's will. I thought you would have enough sense to let that go. Hanging on to some kind of flower business and winery seems a bit ridiculous."

My father had attempted to weasel his way into my grandfather's business. Although my grandfather had been protective of his daughter, my mother, and set aside a trust for her, he'd hated my father, and they hardly spoke for years before my grandfather passed. I should've known my father had someone look into the will. He would've wanted to see if there was any way for him to take advantage.

A bolt of defensiveness hit me. My father knew nothing of Anna and how much she loved that place, but I knew nothing I said could make sense of it to him. Fortunately, I was under no pressure to explain. I simply shrugged. "It's of no importance to you, Father. Nice to see you both."

That was a lie. It was never nice to see them, but I nodded and gracefully turned away. My parents had been neglectful at best. My father had treated me as his own competition once my grandfather took me under his wing. As a result, there was a simmering undercurrent of wanting to one-up my father.

Fast-forward to the end of the evening when I stood on the street outside the main entrance to Jane's flat. She was looking at me expectantly, so I went in. I tried to kiss her, and I couldn't. I lifted my head swiftly before my lips met hers. "I'm sorry," I said as I stepped back.

She looked at me quietly, not seeming the least bit ruffled by my strange behavior this evening. "Have you met someone, Jasper?"

It was on the tip of my tongue to lie and say no, but I surprised myself. "I suppose I have. I can't say I know what to do about it."

Jane regarded me quietly, her lips curling at the corners with a slow smile. "Perhaps you should see what happens. I may not be looking for love, but I'm not immune. You seem out of sorts. If things are not resolved with whoever it is, perhaps you should go see her."

"Why do you assume I would need to go somewhere to visit?" I was genuinely curious.

"Because if you were seeing someone here in London, I would know about it. I think it has something to do with your trip to the States. Some people are best left as part of the past while others leave us wondering. That's what you need to ask yourself. Can you walk away and not wonder for the rest of your life?"

Chapter Thirty-Four

ANNA

I didn't miss Jasper, not at all. I told myself that as I walked into my grandparents' old house. Thanks to his legwork, I'd been able to pay off the money my grandmother owed on that stupid reverse mortgage. I didn't intend to keep the house, but at least now I didn't have to sneak around like a thief in the very place I'd spent the best years of my childhood.

I walked through the quiet and darkened rooms, and my throat felt tight. I missed Gram, and she wasn't coming back. Sometimes you had to remind yourself of the obvious, especially when it came to losing someone who meant everything.

While I also missed my grandfather, I'd had more years to adjust to his death. He also hadn't been as deeply entwined in my day-to-day life when I lived with them. Gram was stability to me, and I'd felt set adrift since she died. I hadn't realized how much the financial situation was weighing on me until Jasper showed up.

I was going to need to learn some form of mental martial arts to vanquish Jasper in my thoughts. Right then, I looked over at the empty file cabinets and pondered how efficiently he'd gone through all those files.

Just thinking about that caused my heart to squeeze tight. I was missing a guy over files. *Files.*

"You have a task," I said to myself.

I began moving through the house, opening the shades and letting the sunshine in. Dust moats floated in the air, and the space felt strangely quiet. I'd arranged for a local homeless services organization to pick up the furnishings, but I still took one last loop through the house. Even though I'd done so when I came here with Jasper, I'd been in a hurry then. I found two old boxes on the top shelf of her closet and nothing more.

I took those with me and was just putting them in my car when the woman arrived to check out the furniture. "Hi there," she said with a bright smile and a cheery wave.

It was a contrast to how I was feeling—out of sorts and missing my grandmother. And Jasper, always missing Jasper. That was freaking annoying.

"Hi there," I replied, managing what I hoped to be a smile. "The furniture isn't new, but it's all in good shape."

When I let her in, she looked around and nodded approvingly. "Looks good. We'll take the stuff off your hands. Are you selling the place?"

"Maybe. I think because of the problems with the foundation, the house itself will be demolished, and I'll figure out what to do with the property," I explained.

That was almost more of a project than I could contemplate at the moment. After she left, I locked up the house and headed back to the winery.

That night, I sat on the couch and started going through those boxes. I hadn't planned to go through them until the lid from one slipped loose and tumbled off as I was carting it up the stairs. Although my hand was healed, I tended to be careful of it and was juggling the box awkwardly when the lid fell off. I discovered the boxes were filled with letters and cards.

Going through them was an excellent distraction, considering that most of my spare time involved me trying not to think about Jasper. There was nothing on to suck me into television tonight, so this would hopefully do the trick.

One box was filled with letters between her and friends. Then I came across the first of some letters from Jasper's grandfather.

For the most part, they were filled with details about daily events. It was the way the letters ended that twisted my heart sharply. *I miss you, and I wish things were different. All my love.*

Tears pricked my eyes as I quickly riffled through the rest of the box. There was a total of ten letters from him, each indicating he'd received one she had written to him. It seemed they had a sweet spot for each other. As far as I could piece together, he'd already been betrothed to another woman when my grandmother went to visit a relative for a summer and met him. My grandmother had already been engaged to my grandfather. I knew she loved my grandfather. That much had been obvious, but apparently, she saved a corner of her heart for Jasper's grandfather.

I wanted to call Jasper and ask him to see what he could find on his end. That made me feel frustrated. We hadn't spoken since he left. By now, it was a point of pride for me. I could be stubborn, so I wasn't going to cave. We had a business arrangement, nothing more.

Liar, liar, pants on fire, my mind taunted me.

Fine, so I was lying. It didn't really matter, and it certainly didn't change the situation.

You're not like your grandmother. You're not promised to anyone, and no one's waiting for you anywhere. Maybe you should try being brave.

Giving my nagging voice a mental kick, I put the letters down. Restless, I stood from the couch, then crossed to look out the windows. It was late afternoon, and the sun was just starting to slide down the summer sky. We were closed today, so it was quiet.

Curling my arms around my waist, I turned away, my eyes scanning the living room. Papers were scattered over the coffee table and on the couch where I'd been sitting. My eyes made their way over to the kitchen area where there were dishes starting to collect in the sink. I'd never turned off the coffee maker this morning, and the blinking red light taunted me.

Dropping my arms, I crossed over and turned the coffee maker off, then began washing the dishes. I felt lonely and annoyed. Until Jasper had shown up and knocked my world off its axis, I'd loved my little apartment. It felt cozy, and all mine. Now, it felt empty because he wasn't here.

After I finished the dishes, I put away the letters, telling myself there was no need to ask Jasper if he had anything like this in his grandfather's things. That was taking sentimental a bridge too far.

I carried the boxes into the now empty guest room. After I put them onto a shelf in the empty closet, I turned and longing sliced through me sharply. My eyes landed on the bed, and I suddenly regretted that I'd stripped the bed and washed the sheets after Jasper left.

Like a foolish girl, I crossed over and lifted the quilt, breathing it in and getting a very subtle hint of his lingering scent. I might've washed the duvet and the sheets, but I hadn't washed the down quilt.

I plunked down on the bed with a sigh. Why, oh why, had I gone and fallen for Jasper?

I stood restlessly again and crossed over to the dresser. I'd never thought to make sure the drawers were empty. They almost were. Except for one thing—a simple hammered silver bracelet. Entirely masculine. Jasper wore it all the time.

As I turned it over in my hands, I noticed an inscription on the inside. It was faded and worn. As I looked closely, my heart thumped unsteadily as I made it out. *To JW from HL. I won't forget you.*

Tears stung my eyes. HL had to be my grandmother, Hannah Lennon. I thought JW had to be Jasper's grandfather since he'd told me they shared the same name, Jasper West. Like me, Jasper had his mother's last name. In my case, it was because my parents had never married. In his, he said his mother kept her maiden name and named him that way by choice. A small detail we shared that suddenly seemed momentous.

Chapter Thirty-Five

JASPER

I reached reflexively toward my left wrist. It was a phantom reflex at this point. The old silver bracelet I'd found in my grandfather's belongings and started wearing because he'd worn it for years was gone. I thought I knew precisely where it was—in Anna's guest bedroom in the dresser. I needed to ask her about it, but that would require reaching out.

At this point, four weeks had passed since I'd left, and I was feeling stubborn. Even though she was across an ocean and a continent, I sensed Anna was being stubborn as well. I missed her *far* more than I missed that bracelet.

"Jasper?"

I looked across my desk at Ben. "Apologies, I'm a little distracted."

He gave me an assessing look, his lips quirking with a smile. "You've been distracted ever since you came back from California."

I shifted my shoulders, willing the tension starting to bundle in my neck to ease. "No, I haven't," I said, my irritable tone belying my reply.

He arched a brow. "We'll pretend you haven't been. I must say, I'm still surprised about your decision."

"What decision?"

"To keep the winery. Are you sure it's not because she wouldn't agree to let you sell? You can fess up if that's the case."

I narrowed my eyes. "No, that's not the case. In fact, she told me if I wanted to sell, she would agree. I decided not to because it's an interesting investment."

"Interesting? It won't make you a penny."

I suddenly felt fiercely protective of Anna. "Don't be so dismissive," I countered. "She was able to pay off the debts her grandmother owed, and it's a solid business."

"Touchy, aren't we? Maybe it will make you some money, but it's nothing like your usual choice of investments. Like your grandfather, I can only assume you have some sort of sentimental attachment."

"What do you mean?"

Ben shrugged. "My only job was to execute his estate, and I feel I've done that. I'm merely saying your grandfather didn't have a logical reason to accept ownership in half of that business, yet he did."

Ben had passed over the letter from my grandfather upon my return. It had simply said he hoped I made the right choice. He was maddening, even in death.

"Do you know if there is any documentation?"

"Regarding what?"

"His relationship with Hannah, Anna's grandmother?"

Ben gave me an assessing look.

"What do you know?" I pressed.

His lips twisted, and he let out a sigh. "He worried it would be misunderstood. He fell in love with Hannah. To my knowledge, nothing untoward ever happened between them. Back then, meeting a girl from America and chasing one's heart simply wasn't done. He was already engaged to be married to your grandmother when Hannah visited London for several months."

"How did they meet?" I interjected.

"I don't have all the details, but I believe he met her when she asked for directions while walking nearby. It was a chance encounter. But he was nothing if not loyal and kept his commitment to your grandmother. I believe Hannah was also already engaged." At my nod, he continued, "After your grandmother passed, he reconnected with Hannah. Helping her was something he could do, so he did."

I stared at him and let out a low laugh. "I suspected it was something like that." Pausing, I ran a hand through my hair. I was grateful to my grandfather because no matter what happened with Anna and me, I would've hated for her to lose the business. It meant so much to her. In that, my grandfather's interference was worth all my internal confusion.

"I'll have my assistant get in touch with you. She has all the paperwork. If there's anything personal in there, you'll find it. Meanwhile, I need to get to another meeting appointment. Meet for a beer at the pub later?"

I nodded absentmindedly.

———

I stared at the faded handwriting on the letter. Anna's grandmother had written about the flowers and when they were blooming, and about her return trip to California after her visit to London that one summer.

She'd written that she was marrying her sweetheart. *I'll never forget you, Jasper. I know sometimes it's possible to love more than one person.*

I could practically feel the tinge of longing in her writing and wondered what my grandfather's letters had said. After my request, Ben had his assistant call me. Before I'd even left my office, a small box of documents had been delivered to my house.

Much of it included the dry details outlining my grandfather's financial investment. In addition, there were a series of letters sent by Anna's grandmother. As far as I could tell from her side of the story, they might have had a chance of being together if circumstances had been different.

Standing from my desk in my home office, I closed the last letter and slipped it back in its envelope. I returned it to the box and closed it. I wanted to call Anna, yet I didn't know if I should. She lived there, and I lived here. Just like our grandparents, it felt as if circumstances weren't in our favor.

Right then, my cell phone chirped from

where it sat on the corner of my desk. Spinning it around, I saw Simon's number flashing on the screen.

"Hello," I said as I lifted the phone to my ear.

"Hello. I didn't expect you to answer," Simon began.

"Why would you expect me not to answer?"

Simon chuckled. "I usually get your voicemail. No need to get fussy about it."

"I'm never fussy," I countered.

Simon cleared his throat in reply.

"Moving along. What can I do for you?" I asked.

"Wondering how things are back in London."

"They're fine."

"Have you talked to Anna?"

I clenched my teeth briefly to keep from swearing. "No, I haven't. Why do you ask?"

"You're being an ass, aren't you?"

"How am I being an ass? Until my trip to California, we'd never met or spoken. Why would we suddenly become chatty with each other? I've known you since I was a boy, and we only talk on the phone every few weeks, if that."

I could practically feel the gleam in Simon's eyes even though I couldn't see his face. He surprised me, though. Instead of mocking me, he said, "Of course. Forgive me for thinking maybe you liked Anna. I think a relationship would be good for you, that's all."

Because I didn't feel like engaging in *that* conversation, I hedged, "How is Bridget?"

"She's great. She's emailing Anna about buying some of that wine she loved so much."

"Ah. Well, I'm sure Anna will be happy to send some."

"I'm sure she will." Simon paused, his voice becoming muted temporarily. A second later, he returned. "Sorry to cut this so short. Brendan needs a little help with his math homework. Bridget says to tell you hello, by the way." Brendan was Simon's stepson. There was no doubt Simon was head over heels in love with Bridget, but if there'd been any question, his dedication to becoming a father to Brendan in marrying Bridget said it all. He'd once claimed he never wanted kids. With Brendan's father having died in a car accident, Simon had fully embraced his role in the family once he fell for Bridget.

"Well, you'd best help him with his math. Please give Bridget my greetings in return."

I got off the phone, feeling annoyed and

envious. Simon was settled and happy with Bridget and his instant family with her son. Not once, not even for a second had I *ever* envied him before.

Now, apparently, I did. I missed Anna, and her casually thrown together gourmet meals. I even missed feeding the chickens and getting my hands pecked and Jasper butting my knees. I wanted to be to Anna what Simon was to Bridget.

I thought about calling her or texting her, or even emailing her in a business fashion. I didn't.

Chapter Thirty-Six

JASPER

"Who?"

"Chance Bateman," my receptionist said.

I could think of no reason Chance would call me, but I was certainly curious. "Put him through," I told my receptionist.

"Hello," I said the moment my office phone buzzed, indicating his call had been put through to me.

"Jasper, glad I caught you," Chance began.

"What can I do for you?"

I wanted to ask him if he'd seen Anna recently and find out how she was doing, but I waited.

"Oh, I don't need anything. I thought I'd call you and let you know Anna is in the hospital."

"What?" I barked.

"Aubrey wasn't sure if you knew, so I dredged up your number and decided to call you. Seeing as you own the winery with her, I figured you might want to know," he explained.

Panic was tightening in my chest, and my breath was short. "What happened? Is she okay?"

"I don't know all the details, but some kind of accident. Apparently, she broke her ankle. They're operating to set it because it's a complicated break."

Chance was far too relaxed and nonchalant about this. "I will be on the next flight to California. Can you do me a favor?"

"Of course."

"Go check on the winery and make sure everything is taken care of. I'm sure with the staff there that all is well, but I'd like someone to confirm. I'll be flying so I won't be able to do it."

As soon as I got off the phone with Chance, I called Anna's number. Rather pointless because I immediately got her voicemail. Fuck.

I called the main number at the winery and got the voicemail there too. Double fuck.

"Is everything all right?" my receptionist asked from the doorway to my office.

Spinning to face her, I shook my head. "Book a flight to San Francisco for me, the fastest and earliest."

Chapter Thirty-Seven

ANNA

"I'll be fine," I said, trying to inject as much confidence and firmness into my tone as possible.

The doctor, who I swore was straight out of medical school with his square glasses and boyish face, pushed those glasses up on his nose and looked skeptically at my ankle. "Ms. Lennon—"

I interrupted him. "Please just call me Anna."

"Anna," he corrected, "you need to be careful. This is a serious ankle break, and I don't want you putting too much weight on it. I'm concerned because I understand you live a busy and active life. I don't want you to change that, but you're definitely going to need to modify how much you're on your feet while this heals."

"I know. I know."

He paused to look down at something on his computer tablet, giving me a moment to try to take a deep breath. Anxiety was coursing through me, and worry was trampling my thoughts.

I had a business to run, and most of what I did involved being on my feet. I was dreading just getting up and down the stairs. As soon as I remembered the stairs, I started trying to figure out where I could sleep downstairs in the winery.

"Now, when can I be discharged?" I asked as politely as possible.

I deserved an award for the timing of this little fall. Last night, after it was dark, I decided to meander down to the winery kitchen because I forgot to bring a bottle of wine upstairs. I fell. After I went back upstairs—being the stubborn fool I could be—and my ankle swelled to the size of a football, I caved and called Eloise. Even though I knew it meant waking her up.

Even though Jasper had set up health insurance for the winery employees—another awesome thing he did—I didn't want to take an ambulance because I knew those could cost a fortune. Because I got to the hospital so late, and they had to operate to put a pin in, they'd kept me for the night. It was now almost evening on the following day, and I was ready to scream.

"As soon as you confirm you have a ride home," the cute young doctor replied as he looked back at me.

"I'll call right now," I said. I started to get up from where I was sitting on a chair with my foot propped up, only to get a stern warning look from the doctor. He didn't look so boyish then.

"Where is your phone, Anna? I'll get it for you. Consider this practice for most of your days for the next few weeks."

I waved a hand toward my purse where it was hanging from one of the hooks by the door. "If you'll just grab my purse, my phone's in there."

The doctor handed me my purse. Just as I was praying Eloise wasn't too busy, there was a light knock on the door to the room where I was waiting.

The doctor called, "Yes?"

"Your patient's ride is here," a nurse said as she poked her head around the door.

The doctor looked at me and then back to her. "Great. Send them on back."

I sent up a silent prayer of thanks to Eloise. She was so on top of it she'd probably already checked in and knew they were about to discharge me. God bless her.

"Be right back," the nurse said.

The doctor was explaining my prescription pain medications to me when there was another light knock on the door. This time when the doctor called for them to come in, Jasper stepped through.

It was a good thing I was sitting down. If not, my knees would've given out, and I probably would've fallen over.

Jasper's sharp gaze met mine, sweeping over me quickly before he shifted his focus to the doctor. "I understand she's ready to be discharged."

Okay, not one word of that was sexy at all. Not even a little. I felt frumpy and cranky, and my ankle hurt. Yet the moment I heard Jasper's crisp accent, my entire body swooned, every single cell. My hormones sent up a hallelujah.

"She's ready to go," the doctor said, oblivious to my internal state of disarray. "You'll need to pick up her prescription for her." The doctor glanced at me, his lips twitching slightly. "She doesn't think she'll need it, but this kind of break can be painful. Make sure she takes it at least at night."

I opened my mouth to protest, but shut it quickly when Jasper sent me something like a glare. "Of course. I'll make sure she takes it at night. Anything else I should know?"

"My medical assistant will give you discharge instructions. She should be fine. We have a follow-up appointment scheduled in three weeks. The most important thing will be for her to stay off that foot as much as possible and to use her crutches at all times to keep weight off it when she's vertical."

"Vertical?" I chimed in.

"Standing up or walking," the doctor clarified.

I had so many things to say, but I couldn't think very clearly. My heart was rioting in my chest, butterflies had burst to life in my belly, and Jasper was here.

Jasper. Was. Here.

Chapter Thirty-Eight

JASPER

My heart was thrashing in my chest, and I wanted to crush Anna to me and kiss her senseless. She had terrified me.

But here we were in this hospital room, and I needed to keep my shit together. First, apparently, I needed to get through the gauntlet of a cute ponytailed medical assistant who was taking this opportunity to flirt shamelessly with me.

"So, you're from London?" she asked.

"Yes."

She batted her eyes, and I looked at the ceiling. It was white and plain. Not a speck of dirt on it that I could see.

When I brought my eyes down again and glanced toward Anna, she was biting her lip to keep from laughing. Bloody hell, I had missed her so much.

After getting through that and picking up Anna's prescription, I turned my rental car down the long driveway that led to the winery. The sun was setting, and the sky was stained lavender and pink. It was beautiful and so peaceful.

The gravel crunched under the tires as I turned into the parking area, stopping beside the path that led into the back of the kitchen. Glancing at Anna, I said, "Don't move."

"Bossy much?" she retorted.

I bit back a smile. We'd gotten through our greetings on the drive back from the hospital, but I was struggling. I'd nearly gone out of my mind over a girl who loved flowers and who had a goat who shared my name. It was just a broken ankle, but I couldn't stop the overwhelming sense of worry and the need to take care of her.

To my surprise, she didn't try to get out of the car on her own. That worried me even more. Because that meant she was in pain.

After I rounded the front of the car, I held the passenger door open, taking her in. Her strawberry curls were mussed, and her brown eyes were tired. "Are you going to let me carry you?" I asked.

Her lips pressed in a thin line. "I have crutches."

"I'm aware of that. I'm also aware getting upstairs on crutches is no easy feat."

If Anna could've snorted and pawed at the ground like an angry horse right then, I was certain she would've.

After a moment, she let out a little puff of air. "I'll use my crutches to get inside, and we'll see how the stairs go."

I fetched her crutches out of the back seat, standing by as she eased her way out of the car. She grimaced slightly when she adjusted one of the crutches under her arm, and worry squeezed my heart. I didn't like contemplating how much pain she might be experiencing.

The doctor had assured me she'd been given pain medication before we left and should be comfortable. Apparently, when it came to Anna, reasonable thought was hard to come by for me.

I walked at her side, keeping my pace deliberately slow. Just as we reached the back door to the kitchen, Jasper and Tinker Bell came trotting around the corner at the winery. Jasper picked up his pace and came charging toward us.

Although he didn't even clear two feet off the ground, I felt the need to protect Anna and stepped in front of her. He promptly head-butted my calves in greeting while Tinker Bell followed at a slower pace.

"Hey there, fellow," I said as I leaned down and scratched between his ears after another head butt. I also greeted Tinker Bell with a few pets and glanced up to see Anna smiling.

"They missed you," she offered.

"Do you think?" I returned as the two little goats meandered along, aiming for the barn.

Anna shrugged lightly with one shoulder. "Maybe. They certainly recognized you."

A sense of warmth settled in my chest. I didn't even want to think about what it meant that it made me happy to consider two silly goats might recognize me.

A moment later, I was holding the door open as Anna crutched her way into the kitchen.

"There you are!" Eloise called as she turned off the faucet at the sink and reached for a towel to dry her hands.

Anna gave her something resembling a

smile. "Here I am. Thank you again for coming to get me last night."

Eloise stopped beside us, resting the towel on the counter nearby. "Of course. You do not need to thank me. I know you would do the same for me. I hope you don't mind I sent this one to get you." She nodded in my direction. "It's been crazy busy here today."

"Of course not," Anna said. Her tone was light, but I sensed a thread of tension there. "It's flower day, so I assumed it was busy. How did everything go?"

"Perfectly fine," Eloise said. "You need to get off your feet." Her eyes flicked down to Anna's ankle, which was in a sturdy boot.

Anna let out a sigh. "I know. I'm going."

"I need to get home," Eloise said. "I'll deal with the goats on the way out. Every-thing else is taken care of, and we're all set for tomorrow and the wine tasting the day after. You rest."

"I'll take care of the chickens and the goats this evening and in the morning," I of-fered as Eloise turned away to hang up the towel.

"Works for me," she replied. After she picked up her purse, she paused and pressed a kiss on Anna's cheek. "You could use this break, so try to take it easy and don't fight it too much."

Anna gave her a resigned smile, and Eloise left. I had Anna's purse in hand as we turned to head toward the back hallway to the stairs.

In an effort to give her some privacy and some dignity, I commented, "I'll be right back. I'm going to use the restroom."

I didn't really need to use the restroom, but I figured this would give Anna a chance to see how the crutches and stairs went. Maybe I was worrying more than necessary. Maybe it would be fine.

A few minutes later, I returned to find her leaning against the wall only three steps up with one of her crutches on the floor at the bottom of the stairs. Her eyes met mine. "This sucks," she announced.

"When the swelling goes down, and you get used to the crutches, it'll be easier."

I picked up the crutch from the floor and took the other one from her before propping them against the wall. I decided against asking her if she wanted me to carry her. Moving carefully, I lifted her in my arms. My heart started pounding because she felt good, and I'd missed her terribly.

She was warm and soft. The boot on her

ankle lightly thumped my thigh as I carried her up the stairs. She was stiff for a moment, but then she relaxed against me. She carried a distinct hospital smell, sterile and disinfected, yet her underlying scent, floral and sensual, broke through. My heart was kicking along against my ribs as I scrambled for purchase emotionally.

I'd just taken a flight in the middle of the night to get back to a girl who'd somehow breezed through all the barriers around my heart. I didn't even realize they were barriers until she kicked them to smithereens with a smile and a silly goat.

Once we got upstairs, I carried her to the couch and eased her down carefully. I reluctantly withdrew my arms away and straightened. "Do you need some extra pillows?"

Anna looked up at me, and I wanted to kiss her. I had to remind myself now definitely wasn't the time. "I have plenty of pillows," she said, a smile teasing the corners of her mouth.

There were plenty of pillows. She didn't skimp on comfort. Her couch was deep with many extra throw pillows scattered on its surface. She reached for several before I had a chance, putting one under her knee and another behind her back.

"I'll go grab your crutches and my bags."

Feeling unsettled and having no idea what to do with the emotions spinning through me like a storm, I hurried down the stairs and out to my rental car. I'd even made sure to get a car with lower clearance for Anna to be able to get in and out of easily.

I grabbed my hastily packed bag and returned upstairs with Anna's crutches in my free hand. I didn't even ask her if it was okay for me to stay in the guest room. I just decided I was. Sometimes, being an arrogant prick came in handy. I didn't dwell long on whether that was okay. It was what I wanted, so it was what I did.

I propped her crutches up on the back of the couch within easy reach of where she sat. "Do you need something to drink or eat before I go take care of the goats and the chickens?"

She eyed me. "If you could bring me my purse and the remote, that would be nice."

As I turned away, I almost tripped over the orange kitten that leaped out from Anna's bedroom doorway and batted at my feet. "Uh, do you have a kitten now?"

Anna laughed a little. "I do. She's harmless although she does like to play. Come here, Mango," she said, reaching for a string of yarn on the coffee table and dangling it.

Mango batted at the yarn and then leapt onto the couch beside her. She promptly started purring madly when she scratched under her chin. "See, she's sweet."

I chuckled, thinking to myself I'd spent more time around animals in the time I'd been in Anna's orbit than in my entire life. I let Mango sniff my hand and then went to get her purse.

After I handed over her purse and got her the remote, I prompted, "Anything to drink or eat?"

"Just some water. I'm not supposed to have alcohol with my pain medication," she offered with a roll of her eyes.

"Water it is." A moment later, I set a glass of water on the coffee table.

I felt more unsettled than I'd ever felt in my life. And that was saying something after my not particularly warm and fuzzy childhood with my parents.

Anna took a sip of the water as I stood there beside the couch. After she set the glass down, she cast a considering look in my direction. "How did you know I got hurt?"

"Chance called me. Of all people," I said with a wondering laugh.

"Oh. I guess Aubrey told him. I'm just a little surprised he called you."

I shrugged. I had a hunch as to why Chance had called me, and not because he chose to enlighten me. As much as he gave off a cavalier attitude about life, it was obvious he was deeply in love with Aubrey. He wasn't the kind of guy to chat or lecture, not like my cousin Simon, but I sensed he was more perceptive than I was about my feelings for Anna.

"You should ask him," I offered. "For now, I'm going to take care of the goats and chickens."

Chapter Thirty-Nine

ANNA

One week later

"Of course, I told Chance," Aubrey replied. She said that as if it were a matter of choice . Which I supposed it was.

"I'm honestly curious," I began, "Do you tell Chance everything?"

Mango was napping on the couch beside me. I idly stroked her through her soft fur. Her presence was a comfort, and she amused me when I was resting, which was just about all I did these days.

"Pretty much," she said, her steady gaze holding mine. "Let's be clear, though, this wasn't like a deep secret. You got hurt. Eloise called me because she was at the hospital with you. It was late, and she needed someone to go check on the goats and the chickens in the morning. She knew you hadn't had a chance to line anyone up. When you ask if I tell Chance everything, if you told me something in confidence like, I don't know, something super personal, I wouldn't tell him. But you broke your ankle. Not top-secret, and I was worried about you. Plus, I left our house at six thirty in the morning. I brought Pixy with me so he could have a little fun while I was feeding the goats. Chance would've wondered what I was doing if I didn't explain."

"I wouldn't have expected you to keep it a secret. I was just curious. I've never really had a serious relationship, so..." My words trailed off, and I shrugged.

Aubrey eyed me from where she sat at an angle across from me on the sectional. "I think you're curious why Chance called Jasper."

I *so* totally was. For just a second, I contemplated feigning nonchalant. But my cheeks got hot, so I knew my blush was giving away my discomfort. I finally let out a laugh. "Fine. You might be right."

Aubrey giggled. "I knew I was right. You

like him. Chance called him because he's got it in his head that Jasper's in love with you. He told me he'd be devastated if he'd found out I was hurt when we weren't together, and he hadn't been able to be there for me."

"What?" I asked, agog at the idea Jasper was in love with me.

Aubrey's eyes twinkled as she smiled over at me. "Is that so crazy?"

"Aside from you, I just didn't know Chance thought that deeply about things. He's a totally nice guy but he's pretty laid-back. Plus, yes, I think it's totally crazy Jasper could be in love with me."

She simply stared back at me, and I felt my cheeks getting hotter and hotter. I started to move my legs restlessly before catching myself. I looked down at my bulky foam boot and cast it a glare.

"What happened with you two?" she asked softly.

I slid my fingers over the silver bracelet on my wrist. "I guess we had a fling," I finally said.

"You *guess* you had a fling?" she pressed.

"Hot sex with no expectations," I finally replied pointedly.

Aubrey threw her head back with a laugh.

"Well, I'm glad it was hot," she said as she finished laughing.

"Well, it was," I muttered. "I thought he was going to stay in London."

"Does it bother you that he cares enough to come back when you get hurt?" she asked.

When she said it like that, it all seemed so silly. It's just, his return had me feeling thrown off balance again. In the weeks he'd been gone, I'd finally started to get my footing back again. Now, he was here, and I just didn't know what to do with my stupid feelings.

I looked over and shrugged. It felt like shrugging was becoming an emotion for me with Jasper. "I don't know. It doesn't bother me. I guess what bothers me is I started to actually like him. But we don't fit, not at all."

Aubrey straightened, looking suddenly serious. "Why not?"

"Why not what?"

"Why don't you fit? I can't say I know Jasper well, but he seems like a nice guy. You already told me he agreed to stay on as co-owner, which makes a huge difference for the business and you. I know you haven't talked about it much, but I know how stressed out you've been. Eloise told me you were worried about having to sell. But that isn't about this, is it?"

I leaned my head against the couch cushions, looking up at the ceiling as though its blank white surface would tell me something.

"No," I replied glumly. "Jasper is a nice guy, but I'm pretty sure he's out of my league."

"Stop it," she ordered, her tone firm and kind of bossy.

Breaking my gaze away from the compelling ceiling, I looked at her. "Stop what?"

"Being so hard on yourself. I didn't think Chance and I would ever have a shot. My God, have you seen him?" She let out a surprised laugh, as if startled at herself.

I smiled in return. "He's not my type, but yeah, he's handsome, but you're totally gorgeous. I'm not talking about looks. Jasper's a rich British big shot. I'm just a girl who's barely scraping by. I feel like a country bumpkin around him."

"When you get out of your own way, is that how you feel when you're with him? I'm not asking for details, but I'm talking about when you're naked," she said bluntly.

I could hear the steady thump of my heartbeat as I recalled how it felt to be held in Jasper's arms. When we were tangled up together, I didn't feel like a country bumpkin. Only when I was thinking. When I was with him, I forgot everything but how absolutely *right* it felt.

"I don't know what to think about him coming back," I finally said, knowing it was a sidestep to her question.

"Well, instead of making things up in your mind, why don't you ask him?"

————

After Aubrey left, my ankle was feeling achy, but I resisted taking any of my prescription painkillers because they made me feel too loopy. I took a few ibuprofen instead and contemplated getting up to do something, anything.

Since Jasper had been here, he'd refused to let me do a thing. Much as I wanted to argue the point, I actually didn't want to spend too much time on my feet. Whenever I did get up and move about, the swelling increased with pain to follow.

That said, I was starting to feel much better, and I hoped I was healing quickly. That evening when Jasper returned after the wine tasting, which I had listened to from a comfortable spot on the couch, I asked, "Why are you here?"

Jasper looked over at me from where he stood just inside the doorway. He closed it, and the sound of the latch clicking echoed in the space. As he crossed the room toward me, his eyes never left mine. It felt as if we were connected by an invisible shimmer of electricity.

He stopped right beside the couch, leaning over to greet Mango when she circled Jasper's ankles. Mango meandered off to look out the windows.

Jasper looked back at me, finally answering my question. "I missed you, and I was worried about you."

I could hear the reverberating thump of my heart as my pulse started to race. I stared at Jasper, almost expecting him to correct himself.

He didn't. He held my eyes, his gaze steady and direct. Heat bloomed through my body. I opened my mouth and then closed it because my brain felt filled with static.

He finally moved, taking several steps and easing his hips down on the couch beside mine. "Here, let me repeat that. I missed you, and I was worried about you," he said in a slow, measured tone, each word ringing like a bell in my heart.

Emotion rushed through me like a gust of wind out of nowhere, sending leaves scattering.

I managed a breath. "I missed you too," I finally said. I might've been terrified by my feelings, but I wasn't going to lie.

One of his hands came to rest on my hip. The feel of his touch was warm, an anchor in the maelstrom of emotion storming through me.

I felt the need to clarify. "I'm okay, though. You didn't need to worry."

Jasper's lips twitched, the smile in his eyes evident. "Maybe not, but I suspect if I weren't here to help, you'd be running around doing too much. The doctor was pretty clear about how you needed to stay off your feet for now."

I wrinkled my nose and sighed. "I know. I am. In fact, I hope you've noticed I've hardly gone downstairs. Thank goodness there's a view up here."

His answering chuckle sent a rush of heat through me. This was inconvenient. I felt anything but sexy right now, but he was sexy no matter what. My body's pull to him was a magnetic force that just wouldn't quit.

"Thank goodness," he said dryly. "I'll help you downstairs whenever you'd like. You know that, right?"

"I know." I twisted my lips.

His smile unfurled slowly. "You don't want to ask for help. You're a stubborn girl. You know that?"

"I'm just used to taking care of myself," I protested.

"I know you can take care of yourself, Anna."

Jasper's hand was still warm on my hip, and his touch moved up the curve of my waist as he lifted his other hand and brushed a loose lock of hair off my forehead. Just that subtle touch demolished my ability to think. Rational thought and reason were replaced with a rush of desire.

His hand slid up over my T-shirt to cup a breast, causing my nipples to pebble instantly. I scrambled, trying to find a sensible thought. "Jasper?" I whispered.

"Hmm?" he murmured right before he leaned over and dropped a hot kiss on the side of my neck.

Because I was shameless and easy when it came to Jasper, and I'd missed him like crazy, I let out a little whimper, arching toward him as he dusted kisses over my skin, scattering sparks in the wake of his touch. "What are you doing?" I finally managed to gasp.

"Kissing you," he said simply.

He nibbled lightly on the sensitive skin behind my ear, and my mind blanked out for a moment. When he lifted his head, I opened my eyes. "You're making me crazy. Is this stupid?" I muttered.

"I promise I won't kiss your ankle," he said with a smile hot enough to melt me.

"I didn't mean that. I meant..." I lifted a hand, waving it vaguely in the air.

"I missed you," he said bluntly. "And you missed me. I see no reason we shouldn't do something about that."

Gah! How was I supposed to use any brain cells when he looked at me like that? I felt like goo inside.

Before my brain could start functioning again... Hell, who was I kidding? My brain didn't function when Jasper was being hot.

He dipped his head, this time trailing a string of kisses along my collarbone. With him, I was frequently discovering new erogenous zones on my body. For example, my collarbone. It felt as if flames were licking across my skin everywhere his lips landed. The heat radiated from my collarbone, sliding through me and turning into liquid need.

Jasper straightened, and I almost whimpered in protest. He lifted my hand where it lay on my belly and dropped a searing kiss in the center of my palm. I was already gone. I'd thrown any pretense about thinking this was a bad idea out the window.

As he looked at me, the air gathered a charge. My heart kept on beating in a wild, unsteady rhythm, and my belly spun in flips. He dropped my hand, lifting his to trace the top of my tank top. Every breath was an effort, and I felt made of fire. And all we were doing was sitting here. I was propped up on the pillows with my bad ankle resting over another pillow on the couch.

Jasper sat beside me, fully clothed, yet the logistics of the moment had nothing to do with how intimate it felt. I knew we had a shared passion, and I knew there were feelings, but we'd never spoken those feelings aloud. For him to say he missed me and for me to admit it in return was momentous.

It made everything feel deeper, adding a layer to the intensity of my physical response to him. It wasn't as if the feelings hadn't existed before. Yet we had shied away from them as though a wild horse had cantered off to ignore them.

This might not've been a smart decision,

but I wanted him too much not to dive into this with him.

"Tell me what you want," Jasper said, his voice deliciously thick.

"You." That single word came out in a breathy whisper.

His eyes darkened as he replied, "Let me do all the work."

How could I say no? Jasper doing all the work meant nothing but incredible things for me. After all, he *was* the man of magic orgasms.

Chapter Forty

JASPER

You.

That single word in Anna's husky voice sent a surge of lust through me. I'd been keeping myself in check for a full week now —telling myself Anna needed to rest, telling myself not to make this about sex, telling myself I was here to help and make sure everything was okay.

After all, I did own half of this business. I wouldn't want anything to happen because she'd been injured. I called bullshit on myself. I could give Anna my half of this business, and it would barely even touch my bottom line.

I was living in delusion because I was terrified of what Anna had done to me. Or rather, what I had allowed myself to feel for her. My God. Without even considering any other complications or ramifications, I'd hopped on a plane and flown here to see her. Over a broken ankle. You'd have thought she'd been about to die based on the level of concern rampaging through me during the entire flight.

Blessedly, there was more than enough to do when I got here. That was about the only thing that kept me sane. Meanwhile, Anna was camped out here on the couch every day, looking cute and sexy as hell in her tank tops and soft, gauzy cotton skirts.

Everything felt electrified. My fingertips rested on her skin just above her tank top, and I was acutely aware of the silky soft feel of her skin under my touch. Her cheeks were pink, and I could feel the rapid, shallow rhythm of her heartbeat under my palm.

I tried to take a breath, but my chest felt tight. Because the only time I felt halfway sane—which was crazy, really—was when I was close to Anna. I dipped my head and kissed her.

Her mouth opened under mine, hot and sweet. God, I fucking loved kissing my girl.

Her tongue glided against mine, and she made a soft sound at the back of her throat.

I let my hands slide down over the curve of her breast, teasing my thumb over her pebbled nipple. Anna shifted restlessly under my touch, her hips bucking slightly, beckoning me. I told myself this was all about her, yet she made me feel greedy. Or rather, my senses were greedy. I wanted all of her now.

I needed to be as careful as possible about her ankle. I told myself I wouldn't be burying myself inside her, not tonight.

I pushed her shirt up, my palm coasting up to cup her breast through her bra. I finally broke free from her mouth. Everything with her was an impossible choice. I never wanted to stop kissing her because she tasted sweet, and I could lose myself in her mouth. But then, I craved the sweet tang of her skin.

I pressed a kiss on the side of her neck, satisfaction washing through me when she arched into my touch and let out a soft, breathy whimper. Lifting my head, I let my eyes trail over her breasts, hidden behind a creamy lace bra with her pink nipples playing peekaboo.

Dipping my head, I sucked a nipple into my mouth through the lace. Her fingers speared my hair. Impatient, I flicked the clasp on her bra undone, immediately turning my attention to her other nipple and teasing until it was a hard peak and she was murmuring my name.

I slid a palm down her good leg. The moment I encountered her skin, I reversed direction, pushing her cotton skirt up. Anna, ever helpful, shifted slightly, her knee falling out to the side.

Lifting my head, my heart seized for a moment when I saw her. Her lips were pink and swollen, her eyes dark with desire, and her skin flushed all over. Her breath was coming in short pants, and she looked downright decadent with her nipples damp from my attention. Her breasts rose and fell with every single breath she took.

I wanted to believe this was about pure need. But lust wasn't what drove me to fly here in the middle of the night. It certainly wasn't what had me feeding goats and chickens and selling wine and flowers. These weren't things I did. Except they were when it came to Anna. Because I would do anything to make her life a little easier.

Her tongue darted out to slide across her bottom lip, bringing me back to what I was doing. She reached her hand over, boldly stroking over my swollen, aching cock.

"I suppose I have to take matters into my own hands," she murmured with a sly smile.

This was for her. Well, selfishly, it was for me too. With Anna, there was a funny quirk to sex. Sex was usually a goal-oriented matter for me. Pleasure being the goal. With Anna, it didn't really matter. Her pleasure was mine.

I caught a nipple with my lips again, releasing it with a wet pop as my hand slid over the curve of her belly. Her skirt was bunched around her hips now. I couldn't resist kissing some of the freckles scattered randomly over her belly.

My hand slipped down over her cotton panties—a quick glance showed me they were pink—and I smiled against her skin as I dropped kisses on the insides of her thighs. She started to move, and I lifted my head, whispering, "Stay still. I don't want you to hurt your ankle."

Anna let out something between a huff and a growl. "Hurry," she ordered.

I chuckled, teasing my fingers over the damp cotton. "We'll see about that," I murmured as I pressed another kiss along the sensitive skin just inside the curve of her hip.

She rocked her hips incrementally into my touch. When she let out a ragged gasp, my restraint snapped from its tether. I just needed to feel her. Pushing her panties out of the way, I delved into her satiny heat.

Getting Anna off with my fingers was pure heaven. I buried one and then another inside her rippling core as one of her hands gripped my hair, and the other clenched her cotton skirt.

Leaning down, I gave her a lazy lick, savoring the salty tang and her ragged cry. I meant to take this slow, but that's not how it went. Not with Anna rocking into me, not with the taste of her arousal dancing across my tongue, not with her voice murmuring my name as she trembled and clamped around my fingers.

Before I knew it, I was looking at her with her hair a rumpled mess around her shoulders as she gasped ragged breaths. I watched her fly apart as I teased her deftly with greedy fingers

Before I could even grasp what was happening, she was unbuttoning my fly. "Anna, you don't—"

She shook her head, her eyes holding mine, bossing me with just a look. In another blinding hot second, I felt her palm curling around my shaft, steel hard and aching. I was so close to release it only took a few strokes, and I was spurting in her hand. Bloody hell.

She had me tumbling back to boyhood when I had little control.

But that was Anna. She ripped my control from my hands with a smile curving on her cheeks and those big brown eyes. A look into her eyes felt like a ray of sunshine in my heart.

Somehow, I regained my dignity. After helping clean Anna up and putting her clothes to rights, I tidied up in the bathroom before returning to the living room. She looked up, and it felt as if my heart stumbled and fell. Its beat stuttered and then rebounded into a thundering rhythm in my chest.

"Do you want to watch something?"

Her question was perfectly innocent. It wasn't even late. I did want to watch something, but not for the watching. I wanted that simple time with her.

I felt as if I needed to be careful, not with her, but with myself. I swallowed before nodding as I crossed the room. "Have you eaten?" I asked when I sat down beside her.

She shook her head, and my stomach growled as if needing to make its own needs clear. She giggled. "I guess we're both hungry." Then, she sighed, worry passing through her eyes as her brow burrowed. "I can't spoil you with cooking because I'm not supposed to be on my feet much."

"You don't need to spoil me with food, Anna. Plus, you have. You made dinner last night and the night before."

She smiled slightly. "It's the only time I can be on my feet. When you're busy in the winery, and I'm sneaking. I promise I sat on a stool most of the time."

I chuckled. "Eloise said there was pizza leftover from lunch. Shall I go get it?"

"You sure you don't mind?"

God, it killed me how independent Anna was. She resisted help so hard. I just wanted to give her more and more. I hated knowing that she worried as much as she did. Her entire spirit was generous, yet she struggled mightily to accept any generosity in return.

"Of course, I don't mind. I'm hungry too, remember?"

"Can I throw together a salad?" she pressed.

"You're going to anyway," I countered. "I'll get you set up at the counter with your foot propped up, and then I'll go get the pizza."

She beamed a smile in response, and my heart banged against my ribs. It felt as if it were shaking the cage of my body.

That night, after we had pizza and a delicious salad, I persuaded her to sleep in her bed. Mango slept at the foot of the bed. I fell asleep beside her, and the tenderness echoing with every beat of my heart almost undid me.

Chapter Forty-One

ANNA

"Mom? What are you doing here?" I was so shocked to see my mother and father, my mouth fell open, and I started to get up from the chair where I was seated at a table in the winery.

For a split second, I forgot I needed to be careful about my ankle. "Easy," Jasper called, crossing to me from where he'd been standing at the bar.

His sharp gaze moved from me to my parents. My mother stood in the doorway, taking off a hat. She wore a long skirt and a faded pink T-shirt. Her gray hair was woven into a braid that fell almost to her waist. My father wore battered jeans and leather boots with a concert T-shirt.

For all I knew, they were wearing the same thing they had the last time I'd seen them four years ago. I tried not to sigh, but it slipped out anyway. I could feel Jasper trying to measure the situation.

"Anna!" my mother exclaimed as she hurried over. She enveloped me in a hug. She smelled like flowers and grass.

My father came over at a slower pace, leaning down to dust an absentminded kiss on my cheek.

"How are you, darling?" my mother asked when she stepped back. She looked around the space. "It looks amazing. Where's mom?"

That was the moment Jasper's entire demeanor sharpened. Because yeah, my mother didn't even know her mother died. That was how much she stayed in touch. Jasper didn't say a word, but he came around to stand beside me, his palm resting lightly between my shoulder blades.

"This place is looking sharp," my dad said slowly, nodding approvingly. The last time they'd been here was before the improvements my grandmother made. They didn't know her house had been foreclosed on, and I didn't want them to know I was considering putting the property up for sale.

I finally collected myself enough to respond. "Mom, Gram died."

My mother stared at me, her eyes going wide as her mouth fell open. "What?" she asked slowly.

"She's dead," I said, feeling a little numb inside. "You know she had heart problems for years. She died in her sleep."

"Why didn't you call us?" my father asked.

Anger flashed inside, but it fizzled instantly. It was an old, tired anger. My parents lived such a free-wheeling lifestyle, getting a hold of them was hit or miss, at best. When they had cell phones and enough money to cover the cost of them, I didn't always have their number.

"I didn't have a number," I said. "I tried calling the last one I had, but it was no longer in service."

My mother sank slowly into a chair across from me. "I just—" She rested her elbows on the table and put her face in her hands. When she lifted her head, her eyes were shiny with tears. "I can't believe I wasn't here."

I didn't know what in the world to say to that. I could believe she wasn't here when Gram died. Because they only popped in every few years when they happened to be drifting through the area. I didn't understand my parents. Maybe I never would. They had met young and fallen quickly into a lifestyle of partying and minimal responsibility.

Originally, they had made sense of their lifestyle with philosophical concepts, such as freedom and not being tied down by our capitalist structure. I could understand the perception and was personally supportive of things like universal healthcare and taking care of each other. But, I also supported a little stability and structure to make sure the basics were covered.

My childhood with them had been one of uncertainty and confusion until they finally left me to stay with my grandparents full-time. We lived on three different communes with an ever-changing rotation of adults and families. My father came across as easy-going at a glance, but he had a temper. He wasn't violent, but he could fly off the handle verbally and lost one job after another. His ability to participate in the communal lifestyle of shared labor was limited as a result. I didn't know what my mother would've been like if it weren't for her falling in love with him, but it didn't matter much.

They were still together, and I didn't see that changing anytime soon. "I'm sorry,

Mom. I did try to call and find you." I spoke the truth, but after a few months of trying, I'd dropped it. I had enough to deal with— my own grief and scrambling to get this place back to rights.

My father stayed quiet. He was an expert at not communicating when things got uncomfortable. After a few moments of sitting quietly, I asked, "Can I get you anything to eat or drink?"

"I don't feel much like eating," my mother said. "Not now. I'll take a glass of water."

My father replied, "Water sounds good. If you've got anything to eat, I'll take it." He finally sat down beside my mother.

Without a word, Jasper's hand dropped from my shoulders as he strode toward the kitchen. Only then did my mother's eyes land on the crutches leaning against the wall beside me and my foot in its supportive boot propped up on a chair. "Oh, dear! What happened?" She glanced over her shoulder just as Jasper disappeared through the door behind the bar into the kitchen. "And who is that?"

"That's Jasper. His grandfather knew Gram and invested in the winery before she passed away. Like I inherited the winery, so did he. As for my ankle, well, I tripped on the stairs and broke it. That's it."

For once, my mother focused more on my well-being. "Oh, hon, I'm so sorry. We're only gonna be here for tonight, but I'll help out as much as I can."

I managed not to roll my eyes. I had zero expectations for my parents, and I certainly didn't need help for one night. Even though I had long ago given up on my parents, I still experienced a twinge of sadness and disappointment. I thought maybe there would be more than a few minutes of sadness over Gram from my mother. My father had never been close to her, so I didn't expect it from him.

When I was a little girl, I had this idea that one day my mom would wake up and realize my dad was kind of a drag, and she would change and be more like her mom. She was loving, but honestly, I didn't know. I guessed the emotional neglect she experienced from my father just sucked that capacity right out of her.

"It'll be fine. With Jasper here, he's taking care of most things. I also have Eloise and the rest of the staff. Everyone helps," I offered.

Jasper returned from the kitchen, actually carrying a tray. I almost laughed. He placed two waters down for my parents and a plate with pizza for my father. I figured he must've zapped it in the microwave to get back that quickly.

He set the empty tray down on a table nearby before sitting down beside me. He was quiet, but I could feel an intensity to him and couldn't help but wonder what he thought of my parents' out of the blue arrival.

My mother looked over at him. "Well, I hear you own half the winery with my daughter. I do hope you're a good partner," she said, almost pointedly, like she had some right to have an opinion.

"Mom, Jasper has been nothing but helpful," I interjected.

"I would hope so," my father cut in, his tone a little sullen. "You inherited a valuable place."

Okay, I was all done with this ridiculousness. "Dad, don't be a jerk. Gram was in over her head with debt, in large part due to how much she helped you two out over the years. She poured her savings into one thing after another for both of you. If it weren't for her partnership with Jasper's grandfather, she would've lost everything. As it was, her house went into foreclosure."

My mother gasped, her palm pressing against her chest. "Are you serious?"

"Yes, mom. I'm serious. Jasper's been nothing but helpful." I turned and looked at my father. "Don't even think about trying to pry money out of me or this place. I don't have it to give."

My father looked sort of chastened. After he finished chewing a bite of his pizza, he took a swallow of water and looked from me to Jasper. "All right, then. I just hope he doesn't take advantage of you," my father added.

God, I was so wary of him. My father was not an evil man, but he drifted through life, looking for the next hand-out because he never could figure out how to pull his shit together enough to take care of himself and my mother, much less me.

"Dad, Jasper could buy and sell this place ten times over. He's not taking advantage of me. If anything, I'm taking advantage of him."

Jasper finally broke his silence. "I don't know either one of you, but I can assure you I will not be taking advantage of the winery. I will, however, make sure that you two can't ruin this business for Anna." His words were slow and measured and delivered in that haughty British accent that made my toes curl.

A ruddy flush crested on my father's cheeks, and my mother studied Jasper for a moment.

"Well, we weren't coming here for money. Just to say hello because we love our daughter," she finally said.

Jasper simply lifted one shoulder in a slight shrug.

Somehow, we got through that awkward hour. I thought my parents would've tried to stay the night, but they changed their plans. Maybe because Gram was gone, maybe because Jasper swooped in and made it clear he wouldn't tolerate them trying to take advantage of the situation. My mother fussed over me and my ankle, told me she loved me a few too many times, while my father sulked. After they finally left, Jasper returned from feeding the goats.

He sat down in the chair across from me. I had my laptop open and tapped save on the menu I'd been working on.

Chapter Forty-Two

JASPER

Locks of Anna's hair fell around her face. She'd tied it up in a knot earlier, but it was coming loose. Her eyes were tired, and tension emanated from her.

I'd watched her interaction with her parents earlier and sensed the uncertainty they stirred up for her. I wanted to stay and protect her from that. It was strange how blinding clarity could come from such a brief interaction.

I'd suddenly understood just how much she craved security. Bloody hell, her parents were total flakes as far as I was concerned. Her mother was loving in a careless way. Her father was an ass. I didn't know all the details, but I could see the main plot lines of their relationship. Now, I understood just how much they'd drained Anna's grandmother.

I'd pulled her father aside and told him point-blank not to count on any help from Anna. It wasn't the money that bothered me. It was how they just expected it from her.

There was that understanding that dawned on me today, followed with the blinding truth of just how much Anna meant to me. I loved her, and I would do anything to make sure she had the security she craved.

She closed her laptop and looked over at me. "Have you eaten? You're working too hard, Jasper," she began.

Of course, she began worrying about me. She always put everybody in front of herself.

I stared at her for a long moment, and then the words just walked out of my mouth. "I love you, you know."

Her big brown eyes went wide, and her mouth dropped open in a pretty little O. Her breath came out in a startled puff. "What?" she squeaked.

Reaching across the table, I laced my fingers in hers, rubbing my thumb back and forth over the center of her palm. "I. Love. You."

"Jasper, you can't—" she sputtered.

"I can, and I do."

Her cheeks went pink. Then, she burst into noisy tears. Not exactly what I expected to hear. But, this was Anna, and this was me, so all I wanted to do was make her feel better.

Standing, I rounded the table and knelt beside her. With her foot in the supportive boot, it was too awkward to pull her up in my arms like I wanted. I made do with sliding an arm around her shoulders. She turned and tucked her forehead against my neck as she took several shuddering breaths.

"Was it that bad?" I asked when she lifted her head and brought her gorgeous eyes to mine. With a sniffle, she shook her head. "It just surprised me is all. And, today was kind of weird. My parents always make me feel all crazy."

"I noticed," I said dryly. "It's okay. My parents make me feel a little crazy too."

Anna looked so startled by that comment that I couldn't help but laugh. "True story. You'll meet them someday."

She stared at me. I could see all kinds of stuff spinning in her mind. I might not have been able to technically see in there, but I could practically feel it—little squirrels of thought dashing around as she frantically tried to figure out what she wanted to say.

She wrinkled her nose, a slow smile curving along her cheek. "I love you too. But it's complicated. You live in London." She gestured out toward the flower fields as if London were out there.

"London's closer in the other direction," I teased.

She pursed her pretty pink lips. "Whatever. The earth is round, so eventually, you would get to London."

For the first time today, actually maybe since I'd arrived this time, I felt the tension ease from her as she considered me.

"What are we doing, Jasper? We can't fall in love."

"Too late. I already did."

"But—"

"Anna, I know it's not convenient. I know you just want to feel secure. It doesn't matter where I live. You don't need to worry. We'll figure it out. It can just be us, and we're the secure part."

She blinked her eyes. She took a quick breath and let it out in a shaky sigh. "Okay."

"Just okay?" I was teasing, a little.

My heart squeezed tight when she nodded slowly. "Okay is good. Really good."

She changed the angle of her head and pressed a kiss in the divot at the base of my throat. For just a moment, her lips lingered. Need seized me, sizzling through me like fire.

When she lifted her head, I slid my hand through her silky curls to cup her nape. Because words simply wouldn't do, I fit my mouth over hers. Her lips parted immediately, and I dove into the heat of her mouth.

Chapter Forty-Three

ANNA

Kissing Jasper made me crazy in all the best ways. I shivered all over. His mouth was hungry and sweet, and I couldn't get enough. He could earn medals for his kisses—the perfect balance of deliciously demanding, and then he would ease off and gentle just enough to make me crave more. The result? Me a needy bundle of girl in his lap.

When he drew back, I whimpered a little. His thumb stroked across the sensitive skin on the side of my neck, sending spirals of sensation radiating from that point. His eyes held mine, dark and searching with a tenderness there that nearly brought tears to my eyes again.

I *knew* I had fallen for Jasper, but I hadn't

believed he had fallen for me. The funny thing was he was so grumpy and kind of snooty—that was his default mode—that I knew he wouldn't tell me he loved me unless he did. He was brutally honest. Even if it stung.

My emotions felt stripped raw, but my heart was full, a fizzy sense of joy bubbling over inside. His hand finally slid away, and he straightened. "Let's get upstairs."

"But you haven't eaten," I protested.

He smiled down at me. "I know, but it's too tempting for you if I stay down here. If you want to get on your feet and make me something, you will," he replied with a chuckle that sent a shiver chasing over my skin.

"Eloise left a tray for us," I offered.

"She did?"

A few minutes later, Jasper had carried me upstairs. He ordered me to remain on the couch after getting me a glass of wine when I promised him up and down that I hadn't taken a painkiller today. I waited, sipping a glass of the fresh white wine. Chilled, it offered a burst of bright flavor on my tongue.

"Here we are," he announced as he came through the door upstairs with a tray in one hand.

He set it on the coffee table before crossing over to the kitchen. "Did Eloise make this so you wouldn't?" he asked as he fetched plates and napkins.

She had made a tray of finger foods. Crackers, a variety of cheeses and cold cuts, along with fresh hummus and some kind of cream cheese dip.

When he returned, I answered, "Probably. She won't admit it, though."

Jasper grinned. He handed me the remote before taking a bite of cheese. I turned on a house buying show. That was a secret pleasure we both enjoyed.

After I finished eating and had a few more sips of wine, I looked over at him. "Feelings aside, you know this is crazy, right?"

He took a swallow of his wine before setting his glass on the table and stretching his arm across my shoulders. "What's crazy?"

"Us. Trying to be in love."

"Anna, there is no try. It's already happened. I don't think it's crazy. Not at all. I think our grandparents conspired to make this happen, and we were lucky."

I gasped. "Oh, my God! I forgot to tell you about the letters I found."

I moved to get up, but he placed his free hand on my thigh. "You're not going anywhere. I forgot the same thing. I have letters. I brought them with me."

After I told him where my grandmother's letters were, he went to get those and fetch the ones he brought with him. Then we sat on the couch and compared.

"So, they were in love. Do you think?" I asked.

"I think. But they were both already promised to others. It looks like your grandmother loved your grandfather very much," he replied.

"I think so. What about your grandparents?"

Jasper shrugged. "I think so too. I'm no expert on love, but sometimes things don't always work out. It doesn't mean the worst. Maybe this was their vicarious attempt to make it work in another time."

"Do you really think they planned this?" I asked, looking into his eyes.

When he stared back, my belly fluttered, and my thoughts derailed. Because, yeah, I had it *that* bad. All I had to do was look at him.

"Perhaps we're giving them too much credit. Clearly, my grandfather was willing to help when things got difficult. He also had a mischievous streak about ten miles wide. I think he wanted to roll the dice and see what happened."

I had another sudden recollection. "Your bracelet! You left it here. Was that your grandfather's?"

He nodded slowly. "Where is it?"

"In the desk drawer," I said, gesturing to the desk.

After he brought it back, he handed it to me when I held my palm out. "Look," I said, sliding my finger over the inscription. "You have your grandfather's name, right?"

He leaned over. "I saw that before but wasn't sure who it was from. I should've connected the dots once I knew your grandmother's name."

Chapter Forty-Four

ANNA

Six weeks later

"Now," Jasper whispered.

Even at a whisper, his tone was deliciously demanding. I was more than happy to obey. With the press of his fingers on my hip as he gave me a subtle tug, I sank down over him, inch by thick inch. I let out a happy hum when he nudged deeper, filling me completely.

"Anna, look at me."

I felt intoxicated with pleasure rippling through me. Dragging my eyes open, I found Jasper's hot gaze waiting. "I love you," he murmured.

My forehead fell to his, my words a whisper against his lips. "Love you too."

We were celebrating because I'd gotten my boot off the day before. It was good, oh-so-good with us. Moments later, pleasure exploded through me. Ever since I told him I had an IUD, we'd skipped the condoms. When I collapsed against him, I felt the heat of his release fill me.

Being held by Jasper was decadent. His muscled arms held me strong, his chest heaving against mine. I eventually lifted my head. He brushed the damp locks of hair away from my face.

"Come to London with me."

That old anxiety started to kick up a storm in my mind. Then he trailed his knuckles across my cheek. "I already talked to Eloise. You need to hire someone else anyway. I'm not suggesting we stay there full-time. I'm just asking you to come with me and see my world."

Jasper had this crazy effect on me where I could actually forget my tendency to worry and think everything was going to fall apart and change in a heartbeat.

"Okay," I whispered.

"Just okay?"

"Okay is good."

He smiled before lifting me off his lap and carting me into the shower.

EPILOGUE

Jasper

Two years later

I was standing there, minding my own business and talking to Eloise. "I'm sure it'll be fine. As long as—"

I was interrupted when Tinker Bell and Jasper came running from around the winery. Jasper hit me straight in the back of the knees and let out what I was positive was his version of a laugh before he kicked his back feet up in the air and trotted off. Tinker Bell stopped for me to give her a pat before hurrying on.

I looked at Eloise and shook my head. "He'll never stop, will he?"

"You're his favorite human. He's like a little boy who has a crush on a girl."

Anna came around the corner. She was wearing overalls and a tank top with a cowboy hat. Every thought in my brain scattered like a daffodil blown in the wind. I even forgot Eloise was there as I reached for Anna's hand and tugged her close.

"Wow, you're never that happy to see me," a voice interrupted.

Glancing up, I saw Chance approaching with Pixy at his side.

I still took a second to kiss Anna. Lifting my head, I said, "Well, it's always good to see you, but Anna is my favorite person."

Chance flashed a quick grin. "Of course, she is. Aubrey is my favorite, so I totally get it." Pixy trotted off when he unclipped the lead.

Eloise interjected, "Good to see you, Chance." Her eyes shifted to Anna and me. "I've gotta run. I'll see you tomorrow when I get here for work." With a wave, she hurried off.

Aubrey approached us with their son, CJ, walking beside her. "Hey," she called. CJ broke free from her hand to hurry over and reach for his father's hand. Chance ruffled his hair.

"What brings you here?" I asked as Aubrey stopped beside Chance.

"I totally forgot," Anna said. She nudged me with her elbow. "I told them they could drop Pixy off to stay with Jasper and Tinker Bell. They're going out of town."

"Just for the weekend," Chance clarified.

"We always have room for another goat," I said dryly.

Occasionally, I marveled at the turn my life had taken. If you had told me two years ago I'd be spending most of my life at a winery in California where I helped feed goats and chickens on the regular, I would have definitely said you'd lost your marbles.

As the saying goes, you never know where life will take you.

Anna and I spent a few months every year in London, but we spent the majority of our time here. We could have balanced it the other way, but I'd discovered I was more relaxed here than when caught up in business in London. Since I could manage my business from a distance due to the benefits of technology, it worked.

Chance, being as straightforward as ever, asked Anna, "Are you pregnant?"

Aubrey let out a sigh. "Chance, stop it. You're not supposed to ask that question."

He looked toward her. "I'm not?"

The affection between them was so obvious. Aubrey simply chuckled and rolled her eyes. "No. It implies you think a woman may be showing, which could mean you think she's gained weight. Also, some people like this thing called privacy."

I looked down at Anna, and my heart started pounding so hard, I thought I might crack a few ribs. Anna *was* pregnant, and I experienced an unfamiliar combination of joy and protectiveness every time I looked at her. She was also sexy as fucking hell. Who knew pregnancy could be such a turn on? I'd certainly had no clue until Anna got pregnant. I fucking loved her extra curves and the flush she carried on her cheeks all the time now. I also loved how sensitive her nipples were. Major bonus.

Anna looked from me to Aubrey, her cheeks going pink. "I am. We were going to keep it quiet, but only until next week. I wanted to make it through the first trimester."

Aubrey squealed and hurried over to give Anna a long hug. While they chattered with excitement, Chance caught my eyes. "You know, I underestimated you," he said.

"Pardon?"

"When you first showed up here two years ago, I thought this British big shot could not wait to leave. I thought this whole situation was a total pain in your ass. But, here you are. You love Anna to pieces, and now you're about to be a family man. Are you ready?"

Chance, for all his casual attitude and occasional wacky sense of humor, was a solid guy. He was deeply committed to his family and Aubrey, goat included.

I shrugged. "I'm not sure I'm ready, but I know it's what I want. To be fair, I don't blame you for underestimating me. I used to be—" I paused, considering my words and feelings. "I suppose what I mean is I used to be shallower and more focused on business. Anna is the best thing that ever happened to me, and I would do anything for her. If you have any pointers on parenting, I'll take them. Right now, I'm doing my best not to demand she rest all the time. She won't, so it doesn't really matter what I say."

Chance threw his head back with a laugh. "You'll be okay. You might pray for some sleep, but losing a little sleep is worth it for the best thing ever."

———

"Congratulations! When's the baby due?" Simon asked.

I adjusted the phone against my ear. "Six months, or thereabouts. For the life of me, I can't believe they pick an actual date."

"I know, it's crazy, right? I'm a doctor, and I still think it's wild. They can nail it down pretty close based on the pregnancy and how it's progressing. It's a very educated guess. How are you doing with this? This is big."

My heart flipped over in my chest. Some days, I was overwhelmed with a soaring sense of joy because everything felt good, good in a way I'd never expected for myself. Other days, I was bloody terrified. What if something went wrong with the pregnancy? What if something happened to Anna?

I didn't want to go crazy in Simon's ear, so I took a deep breath and tried to sound rational. "I'm excited and worried. Tell me it gets better."

Simon chuckled. "You're going to stay excited and probably worried, but it does get better. You learn to live with the worry." He was quiet for a beat before adding, "I'm really happy for you, Jasper. I knew you could be more than a workaholic. I just didn't know if you'd figure it out. Anna is good for you."

"You say that every time we talk," I said.

He laughed. "Because it's true. If it's okay with Anna, Bridget and I would love to come out for a visit, maybe a few months after the baby's born. Sometimes it's nice to have a few extra hands when there's a baby so you can get a break."

"You're always welcome."

"Great, nowhow much should we bet on..."

I cut in, "Dude, I lose every bet to you when we're betting on my life these days."

"Yeah, because you got smart and stopped letting money run your life. Although that's easy to do when you have as much as you do," he said dryly.

Simon couldn't see me roll my eyes, but he could hear me laugh. "It's not the money that makes life good."

"Exactly. Damn, I love being right."

"You're not always right," I countered. Notice I didn't argue this particular point.

Anna came into the living room from the bathroom just as I said that. Of course, she looked gorgeous. Her hair was loose, and the curve of her belly was getting rounder by the day. She had taken a shower after a busy day with the flowers.

"Good to chat, I'll call you soon," I said, abruptly ending my call with Simon.

"Who's not always right?" Anna asked as she stopped to fill a glass of water by the sink.

Crossing over to her, I rested my hands on either side of her hips when she turned to lean them against the counter.

"Simon. He thinks he's always right."

Anna's lips curled in a smile. "What's he right about today?" she asked, her voice a little husky.

I took the glass of water out of her hand and set it on the counter. Brushing some wayward curls off her cheek, I tucked them behind her ear. "He's right that you're the best thing that ever happened to me. I'll give him that."

Anna leaned up and pressed a kiss on the bottom side of my jaw. When she drew away, she said, "Well, you're the best thing that ever happened to me. Did you tell him we were pregnant?"

I nodded, my heart knocking hard in my chest. "I did. I figured if Chance and Aubrey know, I wanted Simon and Bridget to know. We aren't pregnant, you are," I corrected.

"It definitely took both of us," she teased.

Her fingers trailed lightly along my collarbone, sending licks of fire over my skin.

"Good point. Should we practice some more?"

She giggled. "I'm already pregnant. There's no practice needed."

"Oh yes, there is," I murmured as I leaned down to take her mouth in a hungry kiss.

———

ANNA

Ten months later

I woke up slowly, feeling rested for the first time in months. For a moment, I was confused, and then I sat up abruptly in a panic. Jasper wasn't in bed with me, and I didn't know where our little girl was.

My feet slapped the hardwood floors of the new house Jasper insisted we build as I hurried from our bedroom and down the stairs. Skidding into the kitchen, I looked across to the breakfast nook, a round table with a cushioned bench seat tucked into a bay window that looked out over the Pacific Ocean. We'd built this home on a piece of property near the farm, and I'd discovered it was nice to have a little distance as it kept from me working constantly.

Jasper was sitting there with his head leaned against the wall and our little girl sound asleep in his arms. My heart swelled, and I was slammed with a rush of lust.

Jasper made my ovaries do happy dances. Fatherhood suited him incredibly well.

I tiptoed across the room and dropped a kiss on his forehead. I didn't mean to wake him, but his brilliant green eyes opened. "Morning, gorgeous," he said in that gruff British accent.

"Morning. I didn't mean to wake you up," I said apologetically.

"Don't worry about it. You didn't get much sleep last night."

"How is she doing this morning?"

We were speaking in the hushed whispers that parents of babies perfected as a form of preservation. Hannah had been fussy last night.

"Much better." We looked down at her together. "I can probably put her in her rocker now," he whispered.

A few minutes later, after he transferred her into the rocker we kept in the kitchen and she was sound asleep, Jasper crossed over to where I was standing. I hit the start button on the coffee maker and turned to face him.

"Now, where were we?" he murmured as he leaned down and pressed a hot kiss on the side of my neck.

"I don't remember where we were," I said, a little giggle escaping as a shiver chased over my skin.

"Last night," he prompted.

"Ohhhhh." Last night we'd been about to have some sexy times when Hannah started crying.

He held up the baby monitor in his hand with a hot look in his eyes. "Bedroom," he commanded.

It wasn't much later that I sighed in his arms, my skin damp and my body still echoing with pleasure. Lifting my head, I pressed a kiss at the base of his throat. "You started my day off just right."

He held my eyes, his gaze intense. "Every day is just right with you."

I swooned, right there in his arms. I was a lucky girl, the very luckiest.

———

Want to keep up with all of the new releases in Vi Keeland and Penelope Ward's Cocky Hero Club world? Make sure you sign up for the official Cocky Hero Club newsletter for all the latest on our upcoming books:

https://www.
subscribepage.com/CockyHeroClub

Check out other books in the Cocky Hero Club series:
http://www.cockyheroclub.com

ACKNOWLEDGMENTS

Gracious thanks to Vi Keeland & Penelope Ward for inviting me to participate in this project, and to the team at Cocky Hero Club for incredible support in the process.

Many thanks to my editor, to Terri D. for catching the details, and to my early readers.

Always, to my husband and family for supporting me, and to my dogs for keeping me company when I'm plotting and writing.

xoxo
J.H. Croix

ABOUT THE AUTHOR

USA Today Bestselling Author J. H. Croix lives in a small town in Maine with her husband and two spoiled dogs. Croix writes contemporary romance with sassy women and alpha men who aren't afraid to show some emotion. Her love for quirky and relatable characters shines through in her writing. Take a walk on the wild side of romance with her bestselling novels!

Places you can find me & my books:

https://jhcroixauthor.com/books/
https://jhcroixauthor.com
jhcroix@jhcroix.com

Sign up for my newsletter for information on new releases & get a FREE copy of one of my books!

http://jhcroixauthor.com/subscribe/

facebook.com/jhcroix

instagram.com/jhcroix

bookbub.com/authors/j-h-croix